INDIANA JONES™
and the
PYRAMID of the
SORCERER

INDIANA JONES

and the
PYRAMID of the
SORCERER

BY RYDER WINDHAM

LUCAS
BOOKS

Scholastic Inc.
New York   Toronto   London   Auckland   Sydney
Mexico City   New Delhi   Hong Kong   Buenos Aires

ISBN-13: 978-0-545-11205-5
ISBN-10: 0-545-11205-2

12 11 10 9 8 7 6 5 4 3 2 1   9 10 11 12 13 14/0

Book design by Rick DeMonico
Cover illustration by Greg Knight
Printed in the U.S.A.
First printing, May 2009

CHAPTER ONE

*I*ndiana Jones had been enjoying his archaeological dig in Peru before he saw the cheaply printed WANTED poster with his picture on it — an ink drawing of an unshaven man wearing a weathered fedora. The poster had been delivered to him by one of his three Quechuan porters, who had just returned from the nearest village. Examining the poster, Indy said, "Where did you find this?"

"On wall at market," the porter answered. "I take it for you."

"Thanks," Indy said. "Was this the only one?"

"No. Many on buildings. Two on side of bus. And on trees along road." He pointed to the drawing on the poster and said, "He look like you, yes?"

"I look like a lot of guys," Indy said, but the truth was that the drawing looked exactly like him. He was relieved that none of his porters could read. According to the poster, the Peruvian Museum Council accused Dr. Henry "Indiana" Jones,

Jr., of being a *huaquero*, a tomb robber, and the organization had offered a large reward to anyone who captured him alive.

Indy rubbed his chin as he read the poster's text again. The information baffled him for two reasons. First, Peruvian officials in Lima had approved his expedition in their country. Second, and even more disturbing, the Peruvian Museum Council didn't exist.

Someone's setting me up, Indy thought. *But who?*

Before he could ponder this question further, a burst of gunfire sounded from the jungle. Indy ducked instinctively, while his porters suddenly bolted away from the site's camp and fled into the forest.

A few Peruvian officials had known Indy's approximate location but, because his dig was in a remote, isolated area, Indy knew he couldn't have been easy to find. He immediately suspected that the porter who'd delivered the poster had been followed to the site. *Either that or he deliberately led someone here!* Indy drew his own gun from its holster as he dived behind a tree for cover.

"Dr. Jones!" a voice called out from the jungle. In Spanish-accented English, the voice continued: "You are surrounded by Peruvian army forces! You are under arrest for criminal trespass! You will surrender at once!"

When pigs fly! Indy grabbed his green satchel and slung it over his shoulder. He was already wearing his hat and leather jacket, and he had his bullwhip coiled at this belt. Abandoning the camp but keeping his gun out, he sprinted for the trees and onto a path he had cleared.

It was late July of 1941, and Indy was surprised that any Peruvian soldiers would be wasting their time on him. Peru was currently at war with Ecuador, a border dispute that had given him a sense of urgency to complete his work at the small Incan shrine that he had unearthed. Because Peru's army and defenses were far more powerful than Ecuador's, he hadn't been worried about his own safety, but his dig was only about ten miles from one of the more recent skirmishes. As remote as his dig was, it was wildly vulnerable. It made him ill to think about how any battle could instantly reduce a historic site to ruins.

As he plunged down the path through the forest, he heard angered shouts from behind him. It sounded as if at least several men were after him, but he wasn't about to stick around to find out if they really were soldiers. He kept running and didn't look back. He was wondering how determined his attackers were about capturing him alive when another shot was fired. A bullet whizzed over his head, and Indy hoped the shooter had deliberately aimed high.

Less than two minutes later, Indy spotted a tree he had marked with a knife so he would know where to leave the path, which ended in dense foliage after another few hundred yards. He hoped to elude his pursuers by tricking them into following the "false" path. He kept his head low as he weaved between a group of trees and onto another path he had cleared, and he didn't stop running until he arrived at the upper edge of a twenty-foot-wide chasm. The bottom of the chasm was over a hundred feet down.

Although Indy had not anticipated that he would become a wanted man in Peru, he knew from experience that it was always a good idea to have some kind of getaway plan. After he had discovered the chasm, he had taken the precaution of creating not only the paths but also a rope, which he had fashioned from long vines and secured to a branch that dangled over the chasm.

Indy quickly found the end of the rope, which he'd tied to the trunk of a smaller tree that grew nearby. Holstering his gun, he untied the rope's end, picked it up, and gave it a tug. The rope held. He took two steps back, made sure he had a good grip, and then jumped up and swung out over the chasm.

He hadn't noticed the snake that had coiled itself around his rope, just above his right hand. As Indy traveled across the void, the snake slid down the rope and landed on Indy's chest, right between his arms and just under his chin.

Indy had hated snakes ever since he was thirteen years old, and nothing about the specimen that now shifted against his throat was going to change his attitude. Unable to stop his impulse to brush the snake away from his body, he gasped as he removed his right hand from the vine. It was a move he instantly regretted, for as he continued to travel through the air over the chasm, he began to slide down and off the vine. His left hand's fingers dug into the vine and his legs flailed beneath him. Then he lost his grip entirely and fell.

But the vine had already carried Indy to the other side of the chasm, and he landed hard upon a rocky ledge. The snake bounced off him and landed to his left. Indy nearly rolled off the ledge in his effort to avoid further contact with the creature. The snake slithered off and Indy pulled his body away from the ledge. Then he got up, moved away from the chasm's edge, and threw himself down behind a tree. He needed to sit for a moment and catch his breath.

Seconds later, he heard men shouting from across the way. They'd lost him and they didn't sound happy about it. Hoping to identify the "Peruvian forces" who had tried to arrest him, he peeked out from behind the tree and looked back in the direction from which he'd come. A minute later, three men wearing metal helmets and green uniforms emerged across the chasm.

Just my luck, Indy thought grimly. *Peruvian army.*

The vine that had served as Indy's transport now swung lazily back and forth over the chasm. The soldiers looked at the vine, and then peered down over the chasm's edge. Indy hoped they'd think he hadn't made it across. Another minute later, the soldiers retreated back into the jungle.

Still catching his breath, Indy shrugged off his satchel and checked its contents. He quickly confirmed that he hadn't dropped his journal, spectacles, official papers and permits, compact tool kit, leather gloves, maps, or the four small gold figurines — a vulture, a lizard, a fish, and an ear of corn — that he had collected from his dig earlier that morning. Each figurine was only slightly larger than his thumb, and he had wrapped them in protective cloth strips.

Could someone be after the figurines? Indy immediately dismissed the idea. He hadn't even known the figurines existed until a few hours earlier, when he'd been carefully removing dirt from around the Incan shrine's foundation — and he'd told no one about his discovery. He could only imagine who'd buried them there, but would have wagered that they'd been in the ground for centuries. He had recognized the figurines as the symbols of the Mayan deity Kukulcan, the "feathered serpent," and he had intended to take them back to Barnett College in New York, where he was a professor. He hoped that further study would determine how the Mayan artifacts had wound up buried in the Incan shrine.

But all that would have to wait. Indy removed a tattered map of the region and tried to determine how the heck he was going to get home.

His goal was to make it to the coast and gain passage on a ship. Because the Peruvians were after him, he figured he'd have a better chance of leaving South America via Ecuador. There was lot of jungle between him and the coast, but he knew a couple of places where he might catch a public bus. Consulting the map, he plotted a route that would get him across the border, into El Oro, and then to Puerto Bolívar, a port city. With any luck, he could hitch a ride on a banana boat from there.

Indy got up and got moving.

He had no idea that the Peruvian army had already invaded and seized Puerto Bolívar.

CHAPTER TWO

*I*ndy had managed to sneak past the Peruvian soldiers at the Peru-Ecuador border. He had even made it through the war zone and all the way to the docks at Puerto Bolívar and found a boat with a working engine. It was when he tried to leave on that boat that his luck ran out. Three soldiers had been having a secret card game in the boat's cabin and, a moment after Indy started the engine, they had thrown down their cards, grabbed their machine guns, and burst out of the cabin to find an exhausted American man slumped over the boat's controls. Indy was almost too tired to raise his hands, and definitely too tired to resist.

The soldiers relieved Indy of his gun, bullwhip, and satchel, and took him to a nearby warehouse by a stone sea wall that currently served as the Peruvian invaders' command center. Indy was escorted upstairs to an office where he was presented to a Peruvian general. At the general's instruction, the soldiers took away Indy's hat and leather jacket, too. After this was done, the general ordered the soldiers to handcuff the prisoner.

As one of the soldiers snapped handcuffs on Indy's wrists, Jones faced the general and muttered, "I had permission to work in Peru. There are papers in my bag that prove it."

The general smiled, then tilted his nose toward the door to signal his men to take Indy away. As the soldiers hauled him out of the office, Indy glanced back at the general and added, "Careful with my stuff. I'll be back for it later."

The day after his capture, Indy ignored the three flies that were crawling on his whiskered chin while he kept his eyes closed and pretended to be asleep. Fingers laced together, his hands rested across his chest so casually that it appeared he didn't mind the handcuffs that bound his wrists. He was stretched out on a narrow wooden bench, the only piece of furniture within the split-bamboo shanty, which wasn't far from the Peruvians' command center. He had decided that he liked being in Puerto Bolívar just about as much as he liked the flies and the handcuffs.

The shanty was one of many that stood upon stilts above a broad, salty mud flat covered with crushed oyster shells. The ruins of other shanties gave evidence to the battle that had taken place before his arrival. There wasn't any plumbing, let alone fresh water, in Puerto Bolívar, and the stench was beyond awful. The shanty's walls had been lined with old newspapers that did little to discourage invading insects and even less to contain or keep out noise. Indy had had no difficulty hearing the sound of approaching feet on the oyster shells outside the shanty's guarded doorway, and it was this sound that had prompted him to feign sleep.

Indy's eyes remained closed as he heard the door open and shut. Listening carefully, he determined that at least two men, both wearing boots, had entered his makeshift cell. From the clomping sound, as well as too much recent personal experience, Indy had no doubt the two men were soldiers. He began snoring softly.

Something bumped against the sole of Indy's right boot. Indy flinched slightly as he stopped snoring and opened his eyes. He saw two Peruvian soldiers, both wearing metal helmets and soiled uniforms, standing at the end of his bench. The two soldiers appeared relaxed as they cradled their shoulder-slung machine guns. The nearest soldier, a stout fellow with a wide scar on his left cheek, had used his gun barrel's tip to tap Indy's boot. Indy recognized the other soldier as the one who'd placed the handcuffs on his wrists.

Indy yawned. "Can you guys come back later?" he said. "I'm really, really tired."

"*Vamos*," said the soldier who'd tapped his boot.

"Aw, jeez," Indy said as he slowly shifted his legs off the bench and onto the rickety floor. He yawned again. "So much for sweet dreams." He wobbled slightly as he began to rise to his feet. Then he braced both fists together and punched the boot tapper hard in the nose.

It was the best punch that Indy could manage with the handcuffs on. As the soldier's head snapped back, Indy drove his knee up into the big man's stomach, and then swung his fists into the other soldier's jaw. The stout soldier gasped as he doubled over from the impact to his stomach while his comrade crashed onto the wooden bench and landed hard, pinning his own machine gun beneath his body. Indy swung his handcuffed fists again, this time bringing them down on the back of the stout soldier's head. As the soldier collapsed unconscious to the floor, the second soldier — stunned from the blow to his own head — tried to free his machine gun as he grabbed for Indy's left ankle and shouted, "¡Pára!"

Indy had hoped to keep the fight as quiet as possible to avoid alerting more soldiers. With a single desperate kick, he knocked out the second soldier, too.

Indy's heart was pounding hard and fast as he dropped to his knees beside the second soldier and rolled him over. Indy plunged his hands into the soldier's jacket's pockets and quickly found a small box of matches and a metal ring that held three keys. But before Indy could try even one of the keys on the handcuffs, he heard footsteps approaching from outside the shanty's door.

Indy jammed the matches and key ring into one of his own pockets, then seized the fallen soldier's machine gun. As he wrapped his hands around the grip and checked the weapon's safety, he fleetingly wished that one of his captors had been carrying a less cumbersome weapon, a revolver or a machine pistol. A moment later, the shanty's door was kicked open to reveal the two soldiers who had been stationed as guards.

Indy moved fast. He threw his body across the floor so that he lay on his stomach, facing the doorway as he gripped the machine gun awkwardly and fired at the guards. The rapid blasts tore a chunk out of the door and prompted the guards to leap back outside. Keeping his hands gripped on the gun, Indy sprang from the floor and sprinted for the open door.

The two astonished guards had dived to the shell-covered ground outside the shanty. Indy tripped as he exited the shanty and his boots met the causeway, a raised path that was also covered by oyster shells, and the machine gun flew out of his manacled hands. He recovered his balance as he stumbled forward, and his fingers flew out to snatch the gun by its barrel just as the guards began to rise. Taking advantage of his impromptu two-handed grasp on the weapon, he swung it like a club to clip the back of one guard's head and the jaw of the other.

Both of the guards collapsed and lay motionless on the causeway. Indy cast a quick glance around and saw no one else except for a group of nearby buzzards. Dropping to his knees, he set his machine gun aside for a moment as he shoved the unconscious guards under the stilt-elevated shanty.

Indy heard a man barking orders from somewhere beyond the neighboring shanties. It seemed that the sound of Indy's gunfire had not gone unnoticed. However, Indy knew that an armed *gringo* running like blazes through Puerto Bolívar would attract even more unwanted attention. And so he turned and walked away with his gaze lowered to the ground in front of him; he tried to look as casual as a man could wearing handcuffs and carrying a machine gun while strolling through enemy territory.

A buzzard raised its featherless head, looked at Indy, and squawked. Indy's wrists ached, and he hoped to find some discreet place to try removing the handcuffs. He kept walking, weaving between the shanties as he headed for the docks.

Indy's captors hadn't blindfolded him when they'd led him to the guarded shanty, and he had memorized the route so he could return to the warehouse near the stone sea wall. He didn't pause to wonder about whether he had any good chance of recovering his stuff, including the gold figurines, and then stealing a boat and actually getting away this time. If he'd worried about his chances, he would still be stuck in that stinking shanty.

If he did manage to steal a boat, would the Peruvian navy come after him? Indy could only imagine. All he knew was that he couldn't very easily leave Puerto Bolívar by way of the jungle, and he wasn't going anywhere without his gear.

Indy arrived beside some large cargo containers and decided the space between them would be a good temporary hiding place. Propping the machine gun up against one container, he reached for the keys in his pocket. He inserted a key into the hole on his left handcuff and was delighted when it fit. He grinned as he turned the key. When he heard a snapping sound, he thought it was the locking mechanism releasing. But then he saw the key's broken blade sticking out of the left handcuff, and his grin vanished.

Indy heard footsteps approaching. He held totally still, waiting for them to pass. When he could no longer hear the steady crunch of oyster shells, he stuffed the key ring back into his pocket, picked up the machine gun, and inched his way out from between the cargo containers. But as he stepped away from the containers and rounded an intersection between four shanties, he nearly walked straight into a soldier who was coming from the opposite direction.

Without hesitation, Indy lifted his cuffed wrists to aim the machine gun's barrel straight at the soldier. The startled soldier raised his own hands in response. Hoping to move the soldier out of sight and keep him quiet, Indy motioned him toward the door of the nearest shanty. The soldier nodded and took a step backward, but then he lunged at Indy, grabbing the machine gun's barrel. The soldier shoved the barrel aside as he tackled Indy.

Indy's fingers reflexively tightened on the machine gun, and he accidentally squeezed the trigger and sent a spray of bullets into the shanty's stilts as he fell backward upon the ground with the soldier on top of him. Both men held tight to the machine gun. The soldier slammed an elbow into Indy's head. Indy groaned as he twisted his body and drove one of his knees into the soldier's thigh. As the soldier tried to tear the machine gun from Indy's hands, Indy rapidly readjusted his grip, and he winced as the handcuffs bit into his wrists. Using the soldier's strength and position against him, Indy pulled with one hand to drive and brace the machine gun's barrel against the ground, then pushed with the other hand to bring the stock up fast into the soldier's face. The soldier let out an ugly grunt as the stock broke his nose. Indy hit him again and knocked him out cold.

Breathing hard, Indy shoved the soldier's body off of him and scrambled to his feet. A moment later, he heard more footsteps coming his way. He took the machine gun with him as he proceeded at a low trot toward the stone sea wall.

Moving with great stealth, he finally arrived near the warehouse where he hoped to recover his gear. Unfortunately, Peruvian sentries were positioned outside the warehouse's wide-open entrance. Indy held the machine gun in front of him as he dropped and crawled for cover below a shanty, its stilts partially covered by clusters of dead weeds. He'd have to cause some kind of diversion if he wanted to get past the squad, but first he wanted another try at the handcuffs.

He held his hands up to his face and tried to pull the broken key blade out with his teeth, but it wouldn't budge. Then he took out the key ring again to test the remaining keys on the right cuff. The first key he tried fit fine. He gave the key a twist.

Snap!

Indy grimaced at the second broken key.

While failing as a locksmith, Indy had become increasingly aware of the smell of rotting bananas. Shifting his position, he peered through the weeds and spotted an open truck parked on a ramp about fifty feet away from the sentries. The truck was loaded with bananas that had been destined for distant markets before their journey was interrupted by the border war. Judging from the pungent scent that filled the air, the bananas were at least three weeks overdue.

Indy heard more soldiers coming, and he quickly slunk deeper into the weeds. Peering out from his hiding spot, he saw several soldiers run up to the sentries. He couldn't hear every word they were saying, but when he heard *gringo*, he had no reason to doubt that they were talking about him. As he returned the last undamaged key to his pocket, he felt the box of matches he had obtained earlier. Removing the matches, he grabbed the machine gun and crawled to the far side of the shanty.

He positioned himself behind one of the shanty's thicker supports, then tore some dead weeds from the ground and stuffed them up between the structure's thin wooden floor-boards. After doing the same with two more handfuls of weeds, he struck a bunch of matches at once and held them up to the weeds. Once he had a small fire going, he took the machine gun and slunk off below a neighboring shanty until he reached the side of the ramp on which was parked the banana-laden truck.

Indy glanced back to confirm that the fire had not gone out, then slung the machine gun over his shoulder and scurried up the ramp. As he crouched down beside the truck, he noticed that a wooden block had been placed behind the left front tire to keep the vehicle from rolling. He pulled the block out and set it aside, then moved to the back of the truck and lowered the tailgate.

The truck's door was unlocked. Indy opened it quietly and slipped behind the wheel. The keys weren't in the ignition, which was no big surprise. As he released the handbrake, he heard a soldier cry, *"¡Fuego! ¡Fuego!"*

While the soldiers and sentries ran toward the burning shanty, the truck began to roll silently down the ramp, carrying Indy with it. Steering the vehicle while wearing handcuffs and with a machine gun strapped across his back was hardly easy, but Indy wasn't planning a long trip.

None of the soldiers noticed or heard the truck until Indy turned the wheel sharply to the right, causing the tires to screech as he steered toward the warehouse's wide entrance. Rotten bananas flowed over the truck's tailgate, leaving a slippery, foul-smelling trail. Three soldiers turned away from the burning shanty and ran after the truck, but were sent sprawling into the brown and yellow mess that lay in its wake.

Indy guided the truck straight into the warehouse, then flung open the door and leaped and rolled away, letting the truck continue its course toward a far wall. As he pushed himself up from the ground, he heard the soldiers cursing as they slipped in the layers of muck outside. He knew the rotten bananas wouldn't hold the soldiers off for long, so he moved quickly toward the stairway that he remembered from his previous visit to the warehouse.

As Indy ran up the stairs, he adjusted his machine gun so that he once again clutched its pistol grip with both hands. If his gear wasn't still in the room at the top of the stairs, he didn't know what his next move would be. He figured there had to be another way out of the building.

He arrived at the top of the stairs. With the machine gun held ready to cut down anyone who tried to stop him, he threw the door open and burst into the general's office.

Indy found a Peruvian general sitting at a table across from a lean, middle-aged man with gray hair who wore a three-piece suit and a red bow tie. Both men appeared quite startled when they looked up and saw Indy looming in the doorway. The general was holding the WANTED poster with Indy's photograph on it. Indy's hat, bullwhip, gun belt, and satchel were neatly piled on the table in front of an empty chair. Indy's jacket was draped on the back of the chair. Indy thought the man with the bow tie looked familiar.

Keeping his eyes and his gun's barrel leveled at the seated men, Indy kicked the door shut behind him and said, "I'm back for my stuff."

"It's all here," the man with the bow tie replied as he gestured to Indy's hat and the other items on the table.

"General Delgado was just authorizing your release, Dr. Jones."

Indy wondered, *Where have I seen this guy before?*

General Delgado glowered at Indy and said, "Two men, I send for you. Where are they?"

"Taking a nap," Indy said, not feeling inclined to mention the other soldiers he'd knocked out.

Before Delgado could answer, the sound of footsteps charging upstairs came from beyond the closed door behind Indy. Indy moved away from the door but kept his gun trained on the general. From outside, a soldier shouted to the general. Holding Indy's gaze, Delgado replied loudly in Spanish. The unseen soldier gave a short reply, and then came the sound of feet stomping down the stairs as the soldiers retreated.

Placing the WANTED poster on the table, Delgado said, "I tell them everything is under control here. He say you start a fire, but they put it out."

"I'll start a bigger one next time," Indy said.

The man with the bow tie lifted his eyebrows as he faced Indy and said with a strained smile, "I trust our Peruvian friends kept you comfortable?"

Indy suddenly recognized the man. With disbelief evident in his voice, he said, "Musgrove?"

Colonel Musgrove was with U.S. Army Intelligence.

Five years earlier, he had been one of the two government men who had sent Indy to recover the Lost Ark of the Covenant.

Musgrove gestured to the empty chair and said, "Won't you put down the gun and have a seat, Dr. Jones?"

CHAPTER THREE

*F*acing Colonel Musgrove and General Delgado, Indy held his position for a moment. Then he said to Musgrove, "You'll find pliers in my bag and an unbroken key in my left pocket. Help me get these handcuffs off and I might sit for a while."

Delgado watched anxiously while Musgrove removed Indy's handcuffs. When Musgrove was done, Indy continued to hold the machine gun with one hand while he reached into his satchel to make sure the gold figurines were still in it. He was surprised to find that they were, and that they were still wrapped in their cloth strips.

Musgrove said, "There you are, Dr. Jones. Now, please, sit down and put the gun away."

"I only agreed to sit," Indy said, holding on to the machine gun as he lowered himself into the chair. His arms ached, so he rested the gun upon the table, keeping his finger poised on the trigger and the barrel aimed at Delgado.

"This is an outrage!" Delgado exclaimed.

"Imagine how *I* feel," Indy replied through clenched teeth, making Delgado squirm in his chair. Shifting his gaze to Musgrove, Indy said, "So, why don't you tell me what brings you to Puerto Bolívar?"

Musgrove smiled sheepishly and said, "Well, actually, I was in a meeting with some associates in Peru when I read a news item about you being a wanted fugitive."

"Now isn't that a coincidence," Indy said, not believing for a moment that it was.

"Yes, quite," Musgrove said. He tapped the WANTED poster on the table and continued, "After I saw one of these and read that a reward was being offered by the Peruvian Museum Council, I made a few phone calls and found out that there isn't any organization with that name."

Indy snickered. "What a surprise."

"Indeed, it was," Musgrove continued. "Naturally, I was compelled to alert the authorities in Peru as well as Ecuador that the WANTED posters were a hoax, and did everything I could to ensure that you came to no harm."

"Naturally," Indy said. "And I'm sure the general here wasn't at all disappointed when he realized there wasn't a reward for me after all."

"Not true!" Delgado interjected. "I get paid!"

Musgrove shrugged and said, "Well, the U.S. government *is* most grateful to the Peruvian army."

"I bet," Indy said with displeasure. "Now if you're all done with the fairy tales, can we leave?"

Indy had been right about the warehouse having another way out. After Indy put on his hat and gathered his gear, General Delgado personally escorted the two Americans out of the warehouse. Indy couldn't think of any good reason to leave behind his recently acquired machine gun, so he took it with him. Delgado didn't try to stop him.

Leaving the warehouse, Musgrove led Indy to an open car. Waiting beside the car was a young man with short, neatly cut red hair, and a rash of freckles across his face. Although the man was wearing civilian clothes, Indy noticed how his back straightened slightly as Musgrove approached; he pegged the man as an American soldier.

Musgrove gestured to the red-haired man and said, "Dr. Jones, this is Major Nichols."

Nichols extended his hand and said, "How do you do, sir?"

Indy gave a curt nod as he shook hands with Nichols, and then Nichols opened the sedan's back door. Musgrove climbed in and Indy followed. As Nichols got into the driver's seat, started up the car, and they drove off, Indy rested the machine gun across his lap so that its barrel was aimed at the floor, away from Musgrove. Musgrove said, "You really didn't need to take that gun."

"I know," Indy said. "I just felt like it." He leaned back against the seat and tilted his hat down over his eyes.

Musgrove laughed nervously, then said, "You're probably wondering where we're going."

As the car bounced along the causeway, Indy yawned. "Not especially."

Ignoring Indy's comment, Musgrove said, "There's a plane waiting nearby."

"Yeah?" Indy said with feigned interest. "Have a nice trip."

Musgrove was silent for a moment, then said, "I suppose we got off on the wrong foot today."

"Today?" Indy repeated. "Try five years ago, when you and your buddy Major Eaton reneged on your deal with me and Marcus Brody. Remember that deal, Musgrove?"

Musgrove frowned. Choosing his words carefully, he said, "I'm sorry that your, uh, archaeological discovery could not be released to, um —"

"The National Museum," Indy muttered. "They never did get the Ark, did they?"

"But you must realize that decision was beyond my control, Dr. Jones."

Tilting his hat back so it no longer obscured his vision, Indy stared into Musgrove's eyes and said, "What about the decisions you're making now, pal? And how about the ones you made over the past several days? Were all the WANTED posters with my picture plastered on 'em beyond your control, too? And don't tell me you had nothing to do with it. I wasn't born yesterday."

Musgrove cleared his throat, then said, "I admit, I was responsible for the posters, Dr. Jones, and I apologize for that. The simple fact is that I needed to find you, but I had to be discreet about my presence in South America."

Indy shook his head. "So you had the Peruvian army find me for you, and kept your fingers crossed that they wouldn't kill me. Honestly, Musgrove, what kind of sick mind comes up with schemes like that?"

The car swerved slightly, causing Musgrove to slide across the back seat and bump into Indy. Pushing himself back across the seat, Musgrove said, "For what it's worth, the posters weren't my idea, but these are desperate times and it seemed the most expedient solution. I really wish you'd surrendered to the soldiers who found you in Ecuador, as it would have saved us all some time."

"*Saved* us all some time?!" Indy couldn't believe his ears. "*I* was doing just fine on an authorized expedition in Peru before those soldiers showed up and started shooting at me!"

"The soldiers were instructed to fire only to get your attention, not to harm you," Musgrove insisted. "As I said, these are desperate times. In case you hadn't noticed, the conflict between Peru and Ecuador isn't the only war going on in the world. Why, if the Axis powers were to gain a foothold in South America, our own country would be forced to —"

"You're boring me, Musgrove," Indy interrupted. "Save your speeches for someone else."

Musgrove glanced at the back of Nichols's head before returning his gaze to Indy. "Apparently, I can't apologize enough to you, Dr. Jones. And you've made it very clear that you don't trust me."

"That's putting it mildly."

"But the fact is, we need a man with your expertise to help us with —"

"Wait, don't tell me," Indy interrupted again. "You found out about the existence of an ancient relic, something that might be dangerous if it fell into the wrong hands. You want someone to find it and bring it back to you so you can have your 'top men' examine the thing, whatever it is. Due to a total lack of imagination, you think I'm the guy for the job."

Musgrove's left eyelid twitched. "You have some of that right," he said, "except that we *know* it's dangerous, and we believed another man was, uh, 'the guy for the job.'"

"So why didn't you get him?"

"Well, you're familiar with Reginald Brooksbank?"

Indy grinned. "You mean *Sir* Reginald Brooksbank, the world-renowned archaeologist and heir to some fortune or other? Has a home in the Bahamas?"

Musgrove nodded.

"Sure, I know Brooksbank," Indy said. "We go back a ways. He's a smart cookie, Brookie is. I'm not surprised he turned you down."

"But he didn't turn us down," Musgrove said. "Actually, he was the one who contacted us. He was very interested in working with Army Intelligence."

"Really?" Indy said, his curiosity only slightly piqued. "So what's the problem? He backed out on you?"

"No, Dr. Jones. Brooksbank is dead."

Musgrove's words hit Indy hard. He hadn't swapped mail or heard from Brooksbank in a while, but it wasn't all that long ago that they'd been laughing it up at the Explorers' Club in Manhattan. Indy stared at Musgrove with a dazed expression, then blinked his eyes and shook his head. "Dead?"

"Most unfortunate. And I'm afraid the details are classified, a matter of national security. But if you agree to work with us, I can tell you what happened to him, and bring you up-to-date on our current situation."

Indy turned his gaze to look out the window. The sun was shining on the fields alongside the road, for all the good it did.

"I'm sorry I had to break the news to you like this," Musgrove continued. "Brooksbank was a good man. He wasn't an American, but he sure was eager to help us out. I'm not exaggerating when I say that if you picked up where he left off, you'd be helping your country as well as honoring his memory. I just hope you'll consider —"

"Stop the car," Indy choked out.

Thinking his fellow passenger was about to be sick, Musgrove told Nichols to pull over. Nichols did and Indy got out, leaving the machine gun behind. Indy walked a short distance from the car to the side of the road and bent over, placing his hands on his knees as he stared at the ground and took a deep breath.

Musgrove and Nichols got out of the car, too. Musgrove walked up behind Indy and said, "Dr. Jones, are you all right?"

Indy spun and faced Musgrove, his expression fierce. Nichols advanced toward the two men, but Indy glared at him and said, "Back off. This is between me and the old man."

Nichols shifted on his feet, but kept his distance. Indy returned his attention to Musgrove. Indy said, "Let's get something straight. It's not just that I don't trust you. I don't *like* you! Brooksbank was a friend of mine, a *good* friend. And if he died because one of your schemes went wrong, then I like you even less!"

"Dr. Jones, you don't —"

"I also don't like being jerked around," Indy continued, taking a step forward, "especially by some bureaucrat who tries to appeal to my sentimental nature or patriotism. You played me for a rube five years ago, and you didn't score any good points with the WANTED poster business either. I don't owe you a blasted thing, Musgrove!"

"Akashic!" Musgrove said, trying to get a word in edgewise. "Hall of Records! Brooksbank found the Akashic Hall of Records."

Indy laughed. "Oh ho, that's a good one!" When he was done laughing, he said, "You've been duped, Musgrove. The Akashic Hall of Records? The mystical library of all knowledge and ideas in the universe? That old chestnut was cooked up by so-called mediums and psychics years ago, and there's never been a shred of evidence to support its existence. Where'd Brooksbank find it? In your dreams?"

"No," Musgrove said, massaging his stomach as he forced himself to stand upright. "He discovered it in Bimini."

"Bimini?" Indy eyed Musgrove skeptically. "You're serious?"

Musgrove nodded.

"And you have evidence?"

"Yes, Dr. Jones. We do. But that's all I can say until you agree to cooperate with us."

"No deal," Indy said. "Not unless you tell me right now

how Brooksbank died, because I sure as heck don't intend to get suckered into dying the same way."

Musgrove looked at Nichols, and Indy was surprised when it was Nichols who spoke next. "The Nazis killed Brooksbank," Nichols said. "They were spying on him in Bimini, and sabotaged his car to explode. His death wasn't Colonel Musgrove's fault." He paused, then added ruefully, "It was mine. I was in charge of protecting Brooksbank."

Indy's jaw clenched. If there was one thing he hated more than snakes, it was the Nazis. He wasn't sure how to respond to Nichols, but he did appreciate how the young man hadn't minced words or dodged responsibility. Finally, he said, "Did Brooksbank's killers get away?"

"Yes, sir," Nichols said. "I'm sorry."

Indy grimaced. "I'm sure you did your best." Then he looked to Musgrove and added, "Okay. I'm in. But I want to know *everything*."

"If you find the Hall of Records," Musgrove said, "you may very well know everything and *more*."

Confused, Indy said, "Hang on. What do you mean, 'if' I find it? You said Brooksbank found the Hall in Bimini."

"That's correct. But it isn't there anymore."

Even more baffled, Indy said, "What happened? Did the Nazis take it?"

"No." Before Indy could ask another question, Musgrove gestured to the car and continued, "Please, Dr. Jones. I will tell you everything, but our plane is waiting. I hope to reach Costa Rica as soon as possible."

"Costa Rica, huh?" Indy said. "All right, then. But you'd better not forget what I said."

CHAPTER FOUR

*T*he plane that Dr. Henry Jones, Jr., boarded with Colonel Musgrove and Nichols was a Douglas DC-2, without military markings. Just under sixty-three feet long, the twin-engine metal plane rested on a broad expanse of hard ground that currently served as an impromptu airfield. The pilot, copilot, and navigator were American men who, like Nichols, wore civilian attire but had the look of no-nonsense Army servicemen. Musgrove instructed them to fly directly to an Air Force base in Panama, where they would refuel before proceeding to Costa Rica.

The plane's passenger cabin had been reconfigured so that a few seats faced each other with a narrow table that was bolted to the floor between them. Musgrove pointed aft and said, "After we take off, there's a compartment back there where you can get cleaned up, Dr. Jones. You'll also find a change of clothes, and a duffel bag for your own things."

Although Indy still wasn't thrilled about working with

Musgrove, he was relieved to get out of his soiled clothes and have a sponge bath in the cramped compartment. Fifteen minutes later, the plane was airborne and Indy was wearing a clean, white cotton shirt and khaki trousers. He rejoined Musgrove and Nichols, who were seated around the table in the passenger cabin, waiting for him.

A movie projector, a small metal box that resembled a three-inch cube, and a stack of documents now rested on the table. Nichols was busily adjusting the projector's film reels. Musgrove held out a glass of water to Indy. "Thanks," Indy said as he took the water and sat down. After he had a drink, he gestured to the projector and said, "Does your plane also have a popcorn machine?"

"I'm afraid not," Musgrove said. "But we'll watch the film later."

"It better not be *Gone With the Wind*," Indy said flatly, "because I've seen that one before." Eyeing the box and documents on the table, he said, "So, where do we begin?"

Musgrove reached for the documents and said, "When Brooksbank first contacted Army Intelligence, this is what he sent us." He handed a typed letter to Indy, then said, "Notice what he wrote to get our attention, right after his two-sentence introduction."

Indy reviewed the letter. Under Brooksbank's introduction, he found what appeared to be a list of relatively recent newspaper headlines. *Germany invades Crete* . . . Bismarck

sinks HMS Hood ... Bismarck *sunk in North Atlantic ...*
Ex-Kaiser Wilhelm II dies in Netherlands ... British and French
invade Syria. The corresponding dates were typed beside each
event. When he was done, Indy commented, "Okay, so
Brooksbank sent you headlines from late May and early June."

Musgrove said, "Look at the letter's *date*, Dr. Jones."

Indy looked. At the top right corner of the letter, he saw
3 May, 1941.

Musgrove tapped the letter and said, "I will personally
vouch that we received that letter in early May. I have other
documents here, all showing that Brooksbank was able to
accurately predict events."

"Good for you," Indy said. "But that doesn't mean I'll take
your word for it. Papers can be faked, and people can lie. Did
Brooksbank tell you how he found the Hall of Records?"

Musgrove cleared his throat, then said, "He claimed that
a dream led him to its location, in an underground cavern
at Bimini."

Indy said incredulously, "A dream, huh? That's convenient.
An archaeologist living in the Bahamas dreams his way to
possibly the greatest archaeological discovery and it's in his
own backyard. Did anyone else ever see it?"

"I saw the Hall of Records," Nichols said. "Brooksbank
took me there. The entrance was a cave that led to an enor-
mous chamber with a smooth rock floor, and it was lined with
towering columns of light. Brooksbank learned how to gather

information from these columns, and that's how he was able to predict things."

Indy said, "You have any photographs of the place?"

"Only of the cave from the outside," Nichols said, and handed a photo to Indy. The photo showed two clusters of palm trees in front of a rocky wall with a dark opening near the ground. "I tried taking pictures inside," Nichols continued, "but for some reason, they couldn't be developed. All the film negatives were ruined."

"Uh-huh," Indy said, and thought, *That seems very convenient, too.* "So, after Brooksbank was killed, what exactly happened to the Hall? You say it vanished. Do you mean someone destroyed it?"

"No, sir," Nichols said. "It literally disappeared. There wasn't even a trace of the entrance." He handed Indy another photo, this one showing the same palm trees in front of the same rocky wall, only the dark opening was no longer visible. "We confirmed that the entrance wasn't filled by concrete. We brought in some drills and diggers, but they hit layer upon layer of solid rock. It's as if the Hall . . . well, it's as if it never existed."

"You're still assuming that I believe it ever existed at all," Indy said. He put Brooksbank's letter and the photos on the table. "I hope that's not your best evidence."

Turning to Nichols, Musgrove said, "Show him the ball."

Nichols picked up the small metal box from the table and held it open for Indy's inspection. Inside the box, Indy saw a small sphere, no bigger than the average toy marble, which rested on a cushion of dark green fabric. The ball appeared to be made of stone, grayish in color with a slightly crackled surface that reminded Indy of an onion skin. Indy said, "What's this?"

"The only tactile object that Brooksbank ever recovered from the Hall of Records," Musgrove said. "Go on, touch it."

Indy cautiously reached into the box and touched the ball. The moment his fingers came into contact with it, he felt a charge race through his body, and his surroundings instantly vanished. Instead of the plane's interior, he viewed a monolithic statue with outstretched arms that loomed over a lake of lava.

Indy drew his hand back sharply, and suddenly found himself back in his seat in the DC-2, seated with Nichols and Musgrove. Nichols closed the box and placed it back on the table. Musgrove said, "You saw a big lava pool with a giant statue over it, right?"

"Yeah," Indy gasped. "But how?"

"We don't know. Brooksbank couldn't tell us either. All we've been able to conclude about this artifact is that it somehow transmits a very realistic visual image of the statue and lava lake into the mind of anyone who touches it directly. We were hoping you could tell us something about it."

"I've never seen or touched a sphere like that," Indy admitted. "But I recognize the statue. I saw it two years ago, in a chamber below the sea floor, off the coast of Crete."

"At the remains of Atlantis," Musgrove said.

"You heard about that, huh?"

Musgrove nodded. "I read the report written by your partner in the Atlantis expedition, Sophia Hapgood. As I recall, Miss Hapgood had some reputation as a psychic at the time?"

With a slightly embarrassed expression, Indy answered, "Yeah, well, Sophia was pretty good at her fortune-teller routine, but that was before she lost her Atlantean necklace and got her doctorate in archaeology." Then Indy said, "Oh, no," and his eyes swept from Nichols to Musgrove. "Don't tell me you brought Sophia in on this?"

"No," Musgrove said. "We haven't, but . . . is there a reason why we shouldn't?"

"I can't explain it," Indy said, "but whenever she's around, I tend to get shot at more often." Then he looked at Nichols and added, "She's a redhead, too. I hope you're not related."

Nichols responded with a smile. Musgrove said, "Dr. Jones, if Brooksbank's stone sphere transmits an image of Atlantis, I wonder . . . are you aware of any connection between Atlantis and the Hall of Records?"

"None that I know of," Indy said as he scratched his chin's whiskers. "But there may not be any connection at all. I saw

Atlantis with my own two eyes. But the Hall?" Indy shrugged. "Brooksbank's sphere is certainly unusual, and might even be some Atlantean relic, but again, it doesn't prove that the Hall of Records exists. At least not to me."

Musgrove smiled. "So, you still think the Akashic Hall of Records might have been, uh, 'cooked up' by psychics?"

"That's right," Indy said. "Clairvoyants, mediums, fortune-tellers, whatever they want to call themselves."

"You're familiar with Edgar Cayce?"

"Sure, I've heard of him. People say he can communicate with the cosmos, and that he goes into a trance to visit the Hall of Records on some spiritual plane. And before him there was that English guy, died just a few years back . . . what's his name? Lead-something?"

"Charles Webster Leadbetter?" Musgrove offered.

"Yeah, that's him," Indy said. "Leadbetter also claimed he could access the Hall of Records, made it sound like a universal filing system, a place where all ideas and knowledge are stored, not just for the past but the future, too. Every thought anyone ever had or ever will have is supposed to be there."

Nichols said, "But you never believed in it, right?"

Indy lifted his eyebrows, then said, "I'm not saying Cayce or Leadbetter were charlatans. It's entirely possible that *they* believed they'd visited the Hall of Records. But I find it hard to believe in anything that isn't backed up by any physical evidence at all, archaeological or otherwise. You won't find the Akashic Hall of Records mentioned in any legitimate history book."

While Indy took another sip of water, Musgrove said, "Well, I'm sure you'll agree that even legitimate history books don't cover everything. Many books refer to the Royal Library of Alexandria, and yet no one can agree on how or when that library was destroyed."

"Or if it *was* destroyed," Indy added. "Sounds like you've been doing some homework. But the difference is that Alexandria was and is a real place, founded by Alexander the Great around 330 B.C. Try finding anything about the Akashic Hall of Records published before four decades ago, and you'll come up empty. If I remember right, 'Akashic' is just a made-up word, derived from *akasha*, a Sanskrit word for *space* or *sky*. I don't know who coined *Akashic*, but there's no real religion or great history attached to it."

Nichols said, "If I understand you correctly, Dr. Jones, you're basically dismissing the Hall of Records as fantasy because of its association with psychics?"

"Let me put it this way. I've had some bizarre experiences, even seen a few things that I would consider fantastic . . . things that I don't believe will *ever* be explained by science. But when it comes to psychics, I can't overlook the financial angle. The more organized characters go on tours, sell books, and start foundations, which certainly make them seem professional, but none of that proves they have psychic abilities. Maybe it's just me, but until a psychic can tell me exactly how I got this scar on my chin or accurately predict the scores for each game of the next World Series, I'm going to assume every last one of them is a huckster."

Hearing this, Musgrove and Nichols exchanged excited glances, then looked back to Indy. "Fair enough," Musgrove said. "Dr. Jones, it's time to watch the movie."

As a baffled Indy shifted in his seat, Musgrove got up from his seat and walked around the plane's cabin, drawing the shades over the windows while Nichols unrolled a white screen from the ceiling and secured it to a small hook that folded up from the floor. Then the two men returned to their seats and Nichols started the projector. Indy watched the rectangular light flicker on the screen and waited.

Indy felt a sudden knot in his stomach when he saw his old friend Brooksbank appear on the screen. With his wavy blond hair and thin mustache, Brooksbank was a handsome fellow, often mistaken for one famous actor or another. Palm trees and the ocean were visible behind him, and then, by way of the projector, Brooksbank spoke.

"Hello, Indy," Brooksbank said. "I'm on Bimini, not far from my own place. Today's date is July 26, 1941. I *know* you won't believe this, but I've discovered the Hall of Records, right here on this island. Not just discovered the place, but explored it, too. I've set up my motion picture camera to make this movie because I've learned some interesting things from the Hall, things that I must share with you."

Behind Brooksbank, the palm trees swayed slightly as the wind picked up. Watching the images on the screen, Indy realized he'd been unintentionally holding his breath.

"First of all," Brooksbank continued, "the Hall of Records *does* contain information about the future and, so far, all the information has proven to be accurate. However, the future records are difficult to extract, and only seem to yield information for a few months in advance at any given time. For example, as of this morning, I could find no records beyond November of this year. However, I found one more immediate piece of information. I'm going to be killed by Nazi spies."

Indy thought, *Is this some kind of sick joke?*

"I don't know how the Nazis found out about my work on Bimini," Brooksbank continued. "But they will plant a bomb in my car, and I'll die in the explosion. It will happen tonight, and there's nothing I can do to stop it. It's my fate, Indy. Simple as that. But I've also learned that Colonel Musgrove will be seeking you out after my death."

Indy threw a quick glance at Musgrove, but Musgrove's eyes were fixed to the screen. Indy returned his own gaze to Brooksbank's flickering image.

"I want you to go easy on Musgrove," Brooksbank continued. "I know you had some bad business with him before, but trust me, he sincerely regrets what happened with the Ark of the Covenant. I also know that you doubt the existence of the Hall of Records, that you think it's the invention of psychics." Brooksbank grinned at this.

This must be a trick! Again, Indy redirected his gaze to Musgrove. Musgrove returned his gaze, but then looked back to the screen. Indy did the same.

On the screen, Brooksbank's grin faded and he assumed a more serious expression. "Indy, I need to convince you that the Hall of Records is real. And thanks to information I've gathered from the Hall itself, I believe I can do just that. Because now I know what you want to hear. I know the story behind that scar on your chin, as well as the outcome of the 1941 World Series."

Indy's eyes went wide with surprise.

"No, I never asked you about that scar," Brooksbank continued from the screen. "And if you search your memories, you never volunteered to tell me. But according to the Hall of Records, that scar was accidentally made by a bullwhip that you used while defending yourself from a lion on a circus train when you were thirteen years old. It happened on the same day that you obtained your hat."

Indy's jaw fell open.

"As for the upcoming World Series," Brooksbank continued, "you'll have to bear with me on this one, because I confess I never paid much attention to baseball. But here are the facts, which I had to write down." Brooksbank reached into his shirt pocket, removed a slip of paper, and then began reading from the slip. "The New York Yankees will play against the Brooklyn Dodgers, and there will be five games. The Yankees will win the first game 3–2. In the second game . . ."

Mouth still agape, Indy watched and listened as Brooksbank related the score for each successive game. Brooksbank continued, "The Yankees will ultimately defeat the Dodgers 3–1 in Game 5. Now, I realize you'll have to wait for the World Series to verify all this, but I hope that the information about your scar will suffice to convince you that the Hall of Records is real." As Brooksbank returned the slip of paper to his pocket, he said, "Now, Indy, you are thinking, 'If old Brookie can foretell the future and his own death, why doesn't he do something to change his fate?'"

Nichols and Musgrove looked at Indy to see his reaction, but Indy kept his attention to the screen and remained silent. From the screen, Brooksbank said, "You may be discouraged to learn this, but the future is just as mapped out as the past, and it cannot be altered. Any attempt to change fate or alter details in the Hall of Records would wreak havoc throughout time and space. I know I *must* die tonight. I also know that the Nazis will attempt to infiltrate the Hall of Records, here in Bimini, but that they will cause the Hall to vanish. You see, the Hall is capable of transporting itself to different locations. Unfortunately, I'm afraid I have not yet determined *where* it will next materialize."

On screen, the wind appeared to pick up again, whipping at the palm trees. Brooksbank continued, "But I do know this: a stone sphere that I have given to Musgrove is a key to the Hall's next location. You must take the stone to Palmar Sur in Costa Rica, and go to the Three Sisters to find the Hall. You must hurry. I've no doubt that the Nazis will attempt to infiltrate the Hall of Records again, and you have to stop them. They *will* try to use the Hall to their advantage, Indy. From what I've gathered, though I haven't penetrated that particular future, I believe and hope you're the one who can stop them. Goodbye, Indy."

Brooksbank flickered and vanished from the screen, which then went white. A whipping sound came from the projector as the end of the film unreeled. As Nichols turned off the projector, Musgrove said, "I'm afraid that's all we have. Brooksbank left his movie camera in his study. The day after his car exploded, Nichols found the camera and we developed the film — then we went looking for you."

Indy said, "So, now I know why you want to go to Costa Rica. But what was that business about Palmar Sur and the Three Sisters?"

"Palmar Sur is a river town in the Osa region of Costa Rica," Musgrove said. "An American company, Amalgamated Fruit Industries, runs the banana plantations in the area. Recently, some AFI workers were clearing land when they found something interesting."

Musgrove reached for another photograph and handed it to Indy. The picture showed several men in a just-cleared area, surrounded by broken stalks of wild vegetation. The men were holding machetes, and standing beside a large stone sphere that appeared to be over six feet tall. Two other large spheres were visible in the background. Musgrove said, "The workers found hundreds of other stone spheres, but the three pictured here — some locals named them the Three Sisters — are the largest. As you can see, two men are resting their hands against the largest sphere. But so far, there hasn't been any report of these stones transmitting images."

Before Indy could comment, Nichols said, "I found something else besides the movie camera in Brooksbank's study." Nichols reached into his shirt pocket and removed a slip of paper, which he handed to Indy. At the top of the slip were two words: *For Indy*. Below the inscription were the predicted scores for the next World Series. Indy realized he was holding the same slip of paper that Brooksbank had held in the movie.

Musgrove said, "What do you say now, Dr. Jones? Will you help us find the Hall of Records?"

Indy stared at the slip of paper for several seconds before he spoke. "If what Brooksbank said is true, then I really *don't* have any choice in the matter."

But Indy had his doubts, and his mind was racing with questions. *Could the Hall of Records be real? Is there any connection to Atlantis? How else could Brooksbank have known about how I got my scar and hat? And that I wouldn't trust a psychic who couldn't tell me about the next World Series?*

Despite Brooksbank's apparent knowledge and predictions, and despite the existence of the strange spherical artifact, Indy still didn't rule out the possibility that the movie and artifact were elaborate tricks of some kind. Still more questions raced through his head. *If Brooksbank could predict the future, why couldn't he anticipate that the Nazis were watching him? Why didn't he try to contact me earlier?*

Indy could only imagine what the future held and whether the Hall of Records was real, but he was determined to find out the truth.

CHAPTER FIVE

*T*he DC-2 landed at Río Hato, Panama, where the United States Army Air Corps' 32nd Pursuit Group — assigned to protect the Panama Canal — had been based for only several months. From his seat on the DC-2, Indy looked out of a window to see several Curtiss P-36s and some older Boeing P-26 "Peashooters" lined up on the airfield. If the 32nd Pursuit Group had their own insignia, Indy didn't see any sign of it.

Musgrove walked over to Indy and said, "We'll refuel and be on our way to Costa Rica just as fast as possible. I have to send a report to headquarters, but if you want to stretch your legs, this is the time to do it."

"I'd like to get cleaned up and wash my clothes," Indy said. "That sponge bath didn't exactly get the job done."

Musgrove grinned. "That shouldn't be a problem. Nichols will arrange for you to have a proper shower."

Indy gathered his soiled clothes in a bag and was about to exit the plane when Nichols noticed that he was carrying more than dirty laundry. "Your weapons," Nichols said. "You should leave them here. They have a policy against civilians carrying guns on the base."

"What about whips?"

Nichols shrugged.

Hoping to avoid having his weapons confiscated, Indy removed his bullwhip and gun and left them with his satchel in the DC-2's passenger compartment. Then he followed Nichols outside the plane, where a clean-cut serviceman greeted them. The serviceman introduced himself as Corporal McGuinness.

Nichols said, "Is there somewhere Dr. Jones can take a shower and wash some clothes?"

"Of course," McGuinness said obligingly. "This way, gentlemen."

As McGuinness escorted them to a long two-story building, Nichols said, "I'll contact Amalgamated Fruit Industries in Costa Rica and let them know we're on our way to inspect the stone spheres. We should be ready to take off within two hours."

"That soon?"

"Don't worry," Nichols said with a grin. "We won't leave without you."

"That's good," Indy said. "Because I'd have a heck of a time getting my stuff back if you did."

A few servicemen stood talking with each other outside the entrance to the building, but they paid no attention to Corporal McGuinness and the men who accompanied him. Entering the building, McGuinness led Indy and Nichols down a hallway and to a door where he stopped, turned to Indy, and said, "Here's the locker room, sir, and the shower's straight through. We have electric washing machines. Would you like to use one?"

"No, thanks. All I need is a bucket. I'll get everything cleaned up in the shower."

While McGuinness went to get cleaning supplies for Indy, Nichols said, "I'm going over to the commissary to find a newspaper. Shouldn't take long. I'll be waiting out here for you when you're done."

"Fine," Indy said.

As Nichols walked off, McGuinness returned with some soap, a neatly folded washcloth and towels, a wire-handled bucket, and some detergent. Indy said, "Thanks."

"It's a communal shower," McGuinness said, "but it's all yours for now, and the shower was just cleaned. The floor's slippery, though, so watch your step."

"I always do," Indy said.

*   *   *

McGuinness was right: The shower floor *was* slippery. The large, open shower stall was also a bit chilly. Cold enough that Indy wrapped a towel around his waist while he waited for the water to warm up.

Leaving the shower running, Indy stepped out of the stall and back into the adjoining locker room, where he had left the wire-handled bucket and his dirty clothes. He had meant to bring the bucket and clothes into the shower with him, but had forgotten them after he'd gotten undressed and had left them beside a bench in the locker room.

As Indy picked up the bucket, the locker room's door opened and a uniformed man stepped in. The man wore sergeant stripes, had black, slicked-back hair, and was an inch taller than Indy. The sergeant looked surprised to see Indy standing in the locker room.

"Hi," Indy said. "Sorry, I was told I had this place to myself."

The sergeant gave no response, but kept his eyes on Indy as he closed the door behind him. Then he reached into one of his pockets and whipped out a switchblade.

Indy's eyes went wide at the sight of the spring-loaded knife. The man lunged, extending his arm toward Indy's chest, and Indy reflexively raised the metal bucket, lifting it fast to block the blade. The blade's tip struck and deflected off the bucket, and Indy's attacker ended up scraping his own fingers against the bucket's side. The impact also prompted the man to grunt. Before Indy could think of what to do next, the man lashed out with his other hand and struck the bucket with the side of his fist, trying to knock it from Indy's grasp.

Indy gasped as the bucket's handle bit into his fingers, but he held tight to it and ducked as the man drove the blade toward him again. As the knife swept over Indy's head, he gripped the bucket with both hands and then stood up fast, slamming the bucket's rim into the man's head, just below his nose.

The black-haired man stumbled backward, clutching at his nose with one hand while clinging to his knife with the other. Indy swept forward and swung the bucket hard, aiming for the side of the man's head. There was a loud *clang* as the bucket connected with the man's skull.

The man stumbled straight into a wall of lockers, and two locker doors were jolted open as his body bounced off of them. As his attacker slid halfway to the floor, Indy saw that the knife was still in his grip. Indy dropped the bucket and pounced on the man's knife-wielding arm, forcing it into one of the opened lockers and then slamming the locker's door hard.

The man screamed as powder-coated steel struck his forearm with crushing force. He tried to punch Indy's thigh with his free hand, but Indy quickly opened and slammed the locker door on the man's arm again. Although Indy didn't see the man's fingers open and release the knife, the satisfying sound of it clattering against the locker's floor indicated the man had been disarmed.

But he wasn't defeated. The man threw another punch, and this time connected with Indy's rib cage. Indy groaned as he released the locker door and brought both fists down on to the man's head.

Indy almost lost his towel as the man tore himself free from the locker. The man hurled his body forward, away from Indy. Indy thought the man was about to make a run for it, but then the man reached into another pocket.

Fearing that the sergeant was about to extract another concealed weapon, Indy launched himself from the lockers to tackle him. He slammed into the man's lower back and knocked him straight into the shower stall, where Indy's selected showerhead was now sending out a steady spray of hot water. The man hit the shower floor with Indy on top of him, and both men slid across the slick floor until they struck the far wall.

Hot water spattered Indy's bare back as he tried to pin the man to the floor. His assailant still had one hand in his pocket, so Indy quickly rearranged his position to try and immobilize his arms. "Who are you?!" Indy roared, his

voice echoing loudly off the shower walls. "Why're you trying to —?!"

The man twisted his body and managed to drive an elbow
into Indy's sternum. Indy gasped as the man struck him again,
this time so hard that Indy fell off of him. While water continued to spray across the floor, the man rolled away from
Indy, sprang to his feet, and finally removed his hand from
his pocket. Then the man brought both his hands together
and quickly drew them apart, revealing that he had uncoiled a
thin metal wire — a garotte.

Hot water had begun to pool on the floor near the drain.
Indy flung his arm out and smacked the puddle with the edge
of his hand, sending a spray of water up into the man's face.
The man flinched as the water struck his eyes, and Indy threw
himself forward to slam his shoulders into the man's shins. It
was just then, as the man stumbled back against the wall,
clutching at the garotte while Indy tried to knock the man off
his feet, that Indy heard the locker room's door fly open and a
voice cried out, "Dr. Jones!?"

It was Corporal McGuinness. Indy shouted back, "In the
shower! Hurry!"

Indy's attacker kicked at him, but Indy held tight. The
man bent over, trying to snag the garotte around Indy's neck.
Out of the corner of his eye, Indy saw movement outside
the shower.

BLAM!

Indy involuntarily squeezed his eyes closed in response to the almost deafening explosion within the shower. When he opened his eyes, his arms were still wrapped around the man's legs, but now there was blood on Indy's hands. He didn't know if the blood was his own. Both Indy and his attacker looked to the shower's doorway and saw two men facing them. One was Corporal McGuinness. The other was Nichols.

Nichols was holding a small automatic pistol. He squeezed the trigger again, and a second explosion filled the shower.

"No!" Indy shouted. He had hoped to subdue and interrogate his attacker, but Nichols had fired a second bullet into the man who held the garotte. The man crumpled, landing with a wet thud beside Indy.

The man lay motionless on the shower floor while his blood mixed with water and traveled down the drain. Indy reached to the man's throat and tried to find a pulse. He didn't find one.

Indy's ears were still ringing from the gunshots when he looked up to face McGuinness and Nichols. Startled by the sight of the dead man beside Indy, McGuinness gaped for a moment and then said, "Holy cow! What happened?!"

Indy answered, "I slipped."

"The man who attacked you wasn't carrying any identification," Musgrove said. "It seems no one recognizes him."

"Including me," Indy said. He was sitting on a metal table while a lean, bespectacled doctor checked his bare rib cage to make sure nothing was broken. After finding Indy in the shower, Nichols and McGuinness had whisked him to the infirmary and then summoned Musgrove. Over an hour had passed since the fight in the shower, and Musgrove had just been briefed by the base's commanding officer. Now, Musgrove and Nichols watched while the doctor gently prodded Indy's ribs. Indy said tersely, "What about the mystery man's uniform? And how about his knife?"

Musgrove's eyes flicked to the doctor, and Indy took the hint that Musgrove wanted to discuss the situation in private. Musgrove said, "Everything all right, doctor?"

"A few bruises, but I think he'll live," the doctor replied genially as he gently clapped Indy on the back. Then the doctor held out a small metal pillbox. "Want some aspirin, tough guy?"

"Thanks," Indy said, wincing slightly as he eased himself off the table.

Just then, Corporal McGuinness entered the room, carrying a cardboard box. "I've got your clothes for you, Dr. Jones," he said. "Washed *and* dried."

After Indy thanked McGuinness, too, McGuinness and the doctor left the room. Nichols checked the door to make sure no one was lurking outside, and then Indy returned his attention to Musgrove and said, "You were saying?"

"Your attacker's uniform appears to be Air Corps issue. We're checking to see if he brought it with him onto the base or stole it after he got here. The knife was made in Germany."

"So, he could've been a Nazi?" Indy said as he pulled on his shirt. "This is a U.S. military base, for gosh sakes! How the heck did he get past the checkpoints?"

Musgrove shook his head. "No one knows. According to the CO, every gate was and is secure."

"Well, he didn't just materialize out of nowhere!" Indy said. "And how the devil did he know where to find me? Only Nichols and McGuinness knew where I was taking a shower!"

Nichols had his arms braced against his chest, and both hands were balled into fists. "I'm sorry, Dr. Jones," Nichols said. "I failed to protect Brooksbank, and I almost got you killed, too."

"I wasn't accusing you of anything," Indy said.

"I didn't mean to shoot that man dead," Nichols continued. "It all happened so fast. I came back from the commissary, heard McGuinness shouting your name, and ran after him into the locker room. There was a lot of steam, and I guess I couldn't see clearly. I really thought he was holding a gun, that he was about to shoot you."

Indy's brow furrowed slightly. He didn't remember that there had been that much steam.

Nichols shook his head. "I never should have wandered off. I should have stayed with you or posted a guard. If I'd left the commissary a minute later, or if I hadn't heard McGuinness shout —"

"Stop it, Nichols," Indy said. "I'm the one who insisted on taking a shower. Also, that guy snuck past everybody, not just you. As for shooting him dead, he didn't exactly strike me as the surrendering type."

"What's done is done," Musgrove said. "But for now, let's assume that the, uh, mystery man *was* a Nazi assassin." Facing Indy, he continued, "Because he was trying to kill you, we could further assume that he was trying to stop you from reaching Costa Rica, or from finding the Hall of Records."

"Which means he was tracking me," Indy said. "Just how many people knew we were arriving at this base? Besides you two and the crew that flew us here?"

Musgrove and Nichols glanced at each other, then Musgrove replied, "At least eight men in Washington. You think . . . you think someone informed the Nazis about our, uh, mission?"

"What do *you* think, Musgrove?" Indy said. "I haven't even told my own father that I'm not in Peru anymore, and yet a killer with a German switchblade knew just where to find me in Panama. Somebody talked, all right."

Musgrove and Nichols were silent for a moment, then Nichols said, "Maybe there's another possibility. Maybe the Nazis have already found the Hall of Records. Maybe they used the Hall to learn we were heading for Costa Rica, and so they decided to send an assassin to stop us."

"That's a lot of 'maybes,'" Indy said, "and it just doesn't add up. If the Nazis found and used the Hall of Records to predict where we'd be and where we're going, wouldn't they have also predicted that their assassin would fail to kill me?"

"I'm afraid you're right," Musgrove said. "It's more likely that we have a security leak."

Nichols said, "How should we proceed?"

"If we proceed at all," Indy said, "things will have to be different."

"Things?" Musgrove said. "What do you mean?"

"I mean we've tried doing things your way and it's nearly gotten me killed," Indy said. "So from now on, we do things *my* way."

Fifteen minutes later, Nichols stepped out of the examining room and walked to the infirmary's entrance. There, he found Corporal McGuinness facing a nurse who sat behind a desk. McGuinness was in the middle of saying something to the nurse when Nichols interrupted, "Where's the doctor?"

"He just stepped out, sir," McGuinness replied. "But he'll be right —"

"Find him now," Nichols ordered. "And tell him that his last patient wasn't so tough after all."

Confused by the order, McGuinness replied, "I'm sorry, sir, I don't underst —"

"We need to see him immediately. Dr. Jones is dead."

CHAPTER SIX

News spread fast about the death of Dr. Jones at the Air Force base. Musgrove himself, carrying an empty briefcase, went to the DC-2 and informed the pilot, copilot, and navigator that Jones had died of internal bleeding from injuries suffered during a surprise attack. Musgrove then relieved the DC-2's crew and replaced them with three other men, older veteran pilots who'd been personally recommended by the base's commanding officer.

"I want us ready to leave in one hour," Musgrove told the new crew.

The navigator asked, "What's our destination, sir?"

"You'll know in an hour," Musgrove said. Taking Indy's satchel, he abruptly left the plane and returned with his briefcase to the infirmary. But the briefcase was no longer empty.

Musgrove arrived outside the examining room and knocked twice because he knew the door was locked. A moment later, there was a clacking sound as the bolt was released. Nichols opened the door and Musgrove walked in. Another man, wearing an Army-issue shirt adorned with chevrons that indicated a rank of sergeant, stood a short distance away from Nichols, and as Musgrove entered he turned and said, "How do I look?"

"Pretty good for a dead guy," Musgrove said.

Indy grinned. "Yeah, well, just be sure to keep that our secret. You got the stone and all my stuff?"

Musgrove patted his briefcase, then placed it on a table and opened it to reveal the items he had removed from the plane: Indy's whip, gun, and the metal box that contained the small stone sphere. He had also brought a map of the Osa region of Costa Rica.

Indy transferred the briefcase's contents to the larger duffel bag that contained his hat and jacket, and then stuffed his satchel into the bag, too. He said, "Any trouble with switching the pilots?"

"Not at all," Musgrove said. "The commanding officer assured me he'd be keeping a close eye on the crew who flew us here. I still don't think there was any reason to mistrust those men, but the replacement crew is waiting for us now."

"They're going to have a long wait," Indy said, "because we're not going anywhere with them."

"What?" Looking truly baffled, Musgrove said, "But I don't understand. You told me to instruct the crew to be ready to leave in an hour."

"And that's all they need to know," Indy said. "Listen carefully, Musgrove. Right now, there should be only four people on the base who know I'm alive. That would be you, Nichols here, the doctor who examined me, and yours truly."

"You're sure the doctor won't talk?" Nichols said.

"No," Indy admitted. "But when I told him that we're on a secret mission and that I wanted people to think I'd been killed to discourage anyone else from coming after me, he seemed eager to help. Also, I'd trust a good doctor with a secret before I'd trust most other people." Returning his attention to Musgrove, Indy said, "Even though you've removed our former crew from the list of possible blabbermouths, there's still the chance that someone is monitoring you and the DC-2. The plan is to let everyone think that I'm dead, and that you and Nichols will be leaving on that plane."

Musgrove looked from Nichols to Indy, then said, "We're staying here?"

Nichols replied, "While you were preparing the new crew, I appropriated a car and notified the K.O. that a sergeant would drive us off the base."

Indy pointed to the insignia on his shirt and said, "Say hello to your driver." Looking to Nichols, he said, "You got money on you?"

"Sure."

"Good. We'll need it."

Musgrove said, "But . . . where are we going?"

"For a ride," Indy said. "Let's go."

Indy drove Musgrove and Nichols off the base in a somewhat battered Ford military car. From the backseat, Musgrove said, "You're not planning to *drive* us all the way to Costa Rica?"

"You're assuming that I've thought out my plan beyond the next five minutes," Indy said as he steered onto a dirt road and headed east.

Dumbfounded, Musgrove said, "Costa Rica is in the other direction!"

"I know," Indy said. "But I don't like driving with the sun in my eyes, so I'm letting destiny take its course." He stepped on the accelerator to roar past a farmer who walked beside an oxcart.

"This is ridiculous!" Musgrove exclaimed.

"Not if it keeps me alive, it isn't," Indy said as he glanced into the car's rearview mirror. "So far, so good. No one's following us." Looking ahead, Indy saw a sign that indicated he was heading for the nearby town named Santa Clara.

"Dr. Jones, I insist you —!"

"Shut it, Musgrove!" Indy said. "Nobody likes a backseat driver! If you have to know, we're going to Santa Clara. Just a few miles away."

"So you *do* know where you're going?" Musgrove said.

"I never said I didn't," Indy replied.

While Nichols wore a dour expression and Musgrove fumed silently, Indy guided the car over the bumpy road and past a series of small farms until they arrived at Santa Clara, a beach town. Indy scanned several buildings until he sighted a ramshackle cantina that had several cars and trucks parked out front. He pulled over, slowed to a stop in front of the cantina, then turned around to face the two men in the back seat. "I happen to know the guy who runs this place," Indy said. "People call him *el Martillo*, the Hammer, and you don't want to know why. It's been a while since I've seen him, but if anyone can help us get to Costa Rica without being followed, it's him."

Lowering his voice to a whisper, Musgrove said, "This, uh, Hammer fellow. Is he . . . a criminal?"

"He's not beyond breaking a few laws if the money's right," Indy said. "Nichols, let me have the money."

Nichols looked suspicious as he asked, "How much?"

"Well, how much do you have?"

"Two thousand dollars."

Musgrove looked from Nichols to Indy and asked, "Is that, uh, enough?"

Indy whistled, then said, "I don't know how much this is going to cost us, but trust me, the Hammer is not someone we want to offend."

Musgrove said, "You said he was a friend of yours."

"I said I *know* the guy," Indy answered. "Nichols, just give me the money, and trust that I'll try not to spend it all in one place."

"Well, all right," Nichols said as he reluctantly removed a thick envelope from his pocket and handed it to Indy.

As Indy opened the envelope and flipped through the bills, he said, "Do either of you speak Spanish?"

Both Musgrove and Nichols shook their heads. Somewhat embarrassed, Musgrove said, "We didn't think we'd need to —"

"No, no, don't worry," Indy assured him. "It's really good that you don't speak Spanish. I know this sounds crazy, but the Hammer, he's suspicious of American *gringos* who speak Spanish. Thinks the *Yanquis* are trying to take over his business. He trusts me, a little, but it would be a bad move if we all went inside at the same time." Removing a ten-dollar bill from the envelope, Indy handed the bill to Musgrove and continued, "I want you to take this, go inside, and buy everyone a round of drinks."

"Me?"

"Yes, you, Musgrove."

"But why —?"

"Because I want everyone happy when I walk in. Go on. Just buy a round of drinks, and Nichols and I will come in after you."

With obvious trepidation, Musgrove pocketed the bill as he climbed slowly out of the car. He glanced back at Indy and Nichols twice before he pushed the cantina's door open and walked inside.

Indy said, "Nichols, this may be the wrong time to tell you this, but I don't trust Musgrove."

Nichols had been watching the cantina's entrance but now turned to face Indy and said, "You're not talking about what happened with the Ark of the Covenant, are you?"

"No, it's not that," Indy said. "It's something else. Stuff that he said back at the base that just doesn't make sense."

"What?"

"I'll tell you later. If we stay out here much longer, he might get suspicious. I'm going into the bar now." Grabbing his gear as he got out of the car, Indy added, "I want you to wait here for three minutes. If everything is okay, I'll step outside and signal you to come in. I'll just scratch my nose like this." Indy casually scratched the side of his nose. "Got it?"

"Yeah," Nichols said with a grin.

"Something funny?"

"Sorry," Nichols said, "but for a moment there, I thought you were going to suggest that I go into the bar before you, so you could make a getaway with the car *and* the money."

Indy chuckled. "You thought I'd do that? Ha! No, that hadn't occurred to me." Toting his gear with one hand, he held up his other to extend three fingers and said, "Three minutes." Then he walked into the cantina.

A radio was blaring a big band tune that Indy didn't recognize. A Chinese bartender stood on the other side of the bar where Musgrove was seated. Musgrove was surrounded by over a dozen regular customers, mostly native Panamanian laborers, but also a few Jamaicans who were treating Musgrove like their new best friend. A few of the men cast cautious glances at Indy, who was still wearing the sergeant's shirt he had appropriated from the military base.

Musgrove raised a glass of beer to Indy and smiled. Indy returned the smile as he walked up beside Musgrove and said, "Buy these men another round, and then meet me on the other end of the bar. We have to talk. Now."

Musgrove paid for another round and then pushed his way past the grateful customers to join Indy at the far end of the bar, which was near a window and the cantina's back door. Indy said grimly, "How long have you known Nichols?"

Surprised by the unexpected question, Musgrove said, "Nichols? Why, I guess it's been, uh, a little over a year now."

Indy glanced out the window near the back door and saw a pale blue pickup truck pull up and park behind the cantina. He said, "Has he ever given you reason not to trust him?"

"No," Musgrove said. "Why? Is something wrong?"

"Stuff that he said back at the base," Indy said, returning his gaze to the window to see who got out of the truck. "I don't know, it just doesn't make sense."

"Stuff?" Musgrove was baffled. "What stuff?"

Ignoring Musgrove's question, Indy continued, "And just a minute ago, right outside, he *insisted* that I follow you in here. Said he had a hard enough time taking orders from you, that he didn't have to put up with me anymore."

"He said that?"

Just then, the back door opened and the pickup truck's driver walked in. Wearing a Panama hat, he was an older man with dark, leathery skin and a white beard and moustache.

"We'll have to talk about Nichols later," Indy said as he discreetly pointed to the pickup's driver. "Here's *el Martillo*."

"Really?" Musgrove said doubtfully. "Him?"

"Yeah, and don't let his looks fool you. He's tough as the devil and practically owns this town." Taking his gear with him, Indy walked over to the truck's driver and reached out to place one hand on his arm. The man, a total stranger to Indy, looked mildly surprised as Indy gently turned him away from Musgrove. Keeping his voice low and speaking in Spanish, Indy politely offered the man ten dollars to drive him away from the cantina immediately.

The man smiled and answered, *"Sí."*

Indy turned to Musgrove as he gestured to the truck's driver. "Good news," Indy said. "*El Martillo* still likes me. He has an office in the back room. We'll talk there. Nichols won't listen to me, so go tell him to come inside." As

Musgrove started away from the bar, Indy grabbed his shoulder and added, "Don't let on to Nichols that I don't trust him!"

Musgrove had a hard time walking past the grateful customers who hoped he might buy them another drink. When he finally made it through the cantina's front entrance and stepped outside, he found Nichols standing beside their car.

Nichols looked at Musgrove cautiously and said, "Where's Jones?"

"Inside," Musgrove said. "Come on."

Nichols stayed beside the car but shifted from one foot to the other. Because he had been waiting for Indy's signal, he was immediately concerned by Musgrove's appearance. "Jones said . . . he wants me inside?"

"Yes," Musgrove said impatiently. "He found his man and we're going to talk with him in the back room. So come on, let's go."

Eyes locked on each other, Musgrove and Nichols didn't notice the pale blue pickup truck that drove away from the cantina. If they *had* noticed the truck, they wouldn't have seen Indy, who had ducked down in the front seat while he pretended to tighten the laces on one boot. As the truck drove off, Nichols gazed suspiciously at Musgrove and said, "Why are *you* telling me to come in?"

"What's eating you, Nichols?" Musgrove said. "You want me to *order* you to come in?"

"Order me?" Nichols looked at the cantina's door, then back to Musgrove and said, "Did Jones say anything about a signal?"

"Signal?" Musgrove shook his head. "What are you talking about?"

Nichols suddenly realized that Jones was up to something and his freckled face went crimson. He bolted for the cantina's entrance, startling Musgrove as he brushed past him. Musgrove recovered fast and quickly followed Nichols into the cantina. The happy customers loudly welcomed Musgrove's return, slapping him on the back while Nichols ran to the other end of the cantina.

Nichols quickly confirmed that the building didn't have a back room. Wondering where Indy had gone, he muttered through clenched teeth, "The car."

Nichols shoved his way past Musgrove and the customers and sprinted out of the cantina's front door. He had thought that Indy used their car for a getaway after all, so he was surprised to find the vehicle resting where he'd left it. But then, moving beside the car and looking to the dashboard, he saw the empty ignition and realized that Indy had taken the car's keys with him when he'd carried his gear into the cantina.

Along with all the money.

And the invaluable stone sphere.

Nichols cursed out loud.

The blue pickup truck was over a mile away from the cantina when Indy told the driver he was willing to pay ten dollars more if the driver could take him to a pilot who owned a private plane. The driver smiled broadly and said he could do that, too.

CHAPTER SEVEN

Buenas *tardes*," Indy said to the two burly men who sat on a bench in front of the wide, one-storey concrete building where the truck driver had dropped him off. Indy had changed into his own safari shirt and had given his sergeant's shirt to the driver, who was already on his way back to Santa Clara.

Both of the seated men wore dirty work clothes and Panama hats, and there were several empty wine jugs lined up to the left of the bench. A stack of oil drums and a few wooden crates stood beside the building, which looked more like a garage or a bunker than a house. Beyond the building, a long, wide field stretched down to a beach. At the far end of the field was a tall wooden pole that flew a brightly striped wind sock.

However, two other features — a rickety chicken coop, and a clothesline with cleaned white shirts and khaki trousers dangling from it — suggested that someone called the place home. At a glance, Indy could tell the clothing belonged to someone shorter than him.

One of the seated men looked up at Indy with a disinterested expression. The other man, who was slightly smaller than a grizzly bear, gnawed at a roasted chicken leg that he held with his thick, greasy fingers. He gave Indy a cursory glance before returning his attention to his meal.

In Spanish, Indy introduced himself as an American traveler, and then asked the men if either one of them was Bert, for that was the name that the truck driver had given for the pilot who operated out of the concrete building and makeshift airfield.

The two men looked at each other for a moment, and then they burst out laughing.

Indy surveyed the men. "Bert?" he repeated, then thought, *Maybe Bert is a nickname.* "O Albert? O Roberto?" The men laughed even louder. Indy had no idea what they found so amusing, but there was a hint of menace in their laughter, and he wondered if it had been a mistake to leave his bullwhip and gun in the duffel bag that he clutched in his left hand.

Just then, Indy heard an engine whine overhead. He looked up and saw a biplane approaching, heading for the field beyond the concrete house. He wasn't an expert on planes, but he could tell this one had tandem cockpits and didn't look too old. Indy was about to ask the laughing men if they knew the pilot's name, when the larger of the pair quietly stood up, tossed aside his chicken leg, and wrapped his fingers around Indy's throat.

Indy gasped as he brought his right hand up fast, slamming the upturned base of his palm under the big man's jaw. The man had still been chewing on a piece of chicken but the brutal impact of Indy's hand caused him to bite his tongue as his head snapped back. The man released his fingers from Indy's neck, and Indy drove a knee into the man's thick stomach.

The other man got to his feet and glared at Indy. Indy swung his duffel bag at the man, who stumbled back against the bench and fell upon the wine jugs. As Indy plunged his hand into the bag and blindly clawed for his weapons, the larger man — still clutching at his injured jaw — lurched forward and rammed Indy's side with his elbows.

Indy grunted but held tight to the bag as he fell to the ground. Hoping to avoid getting kicked by his attackers, he rolled away from them as his one hand finally seized upon a small, solid object within the depths of his bag. Not sure what the object was but hoping he could use it as a weapon, he pulled his hand from the bag to see that he grasped one of the cloth-wrapped gold figurines he'd obtained from the Incan shrine in Peru.

Indy was still sprawled on the ground when the man he had sent tumbling onto the bench got up and leaped for him. Indy raised his arm fast so that the bottom of the gold figurine connected with the incoming man's forehead. The man was immediately knocked out and collapsed upon Indy.

Indy was so preoccupied with staying alive that he was only dimly aware that the noise of the biplane's engine had grown louder. He shoved the unconscious man off him and wriggled out from underneath, just as the other man drew back his leg to kick him.

Indy rolled as he shoved the duffel bag between him and the bearish man's foot. The bag absorbed most of the impact, but Indy still gasped as he swung the gold figurine straight into the kicker's shin.

The man howled as Indy rapidly scrambled to his feet and returned the figurine to the bag. This time, his fingers found the handle of his whip, and he drew it out fast. The motion sent the tip of his whip out and away from him with a loud crack, and then he sent the lash out at the big man. The whip's end coiled and snapped around the man's left ankle, and Indy seized the whip's handle with both hands and pulled hard. The man fell backward and the back of his head smashed against one of the stray wine jugs. He tried to raise his head, but then his eyes rolled back into their sockets and he passed out.

Indy tugged at his whip again, pulling it free from the fallen man's leg, but then a loud gunshot was heard. Indy flinched and then froze. Cautiously looking around to see where the shot had come from, he finally noticed that the biplane had already landed in the field beyond the building. Its engine was still whining down, and the pilot had left the cockpit and now stood before the garments that hung on the line less than twenty feet away from Indy.

The pilot wore a white shirt and leather aviator helmet with goggles, and held a revolver in one gloved hand. The pilot's gun was aimed at the sky, and Indy realized the shot had been just a warning. But then the pilot lowered the gun so that it was aimed at Indy.

"Drop the whip!" the pilot shouted.

Indy dropped the whip and gaped at the pilot. He had been right about one thing: the clothes strung on the line did belong to someone shorter than him. But he hadn't expected the pilot to be a woman.

The biplane's engine came to a sputtering stop. Keeping her gun trained on Indy, the pilot said, "Who are you, and what do you want?!"

"My name is Jones. I'm looking for a pilot who can get me to Costa Rica. I hitched a ride with a man who told me I should talk with Bert."

"You're talking to her," the pilot answered as she pushed back her goggles with her free hand. "I'm Bert. Bert Brodowski."

"Oh." Indy grinned and shook his head. Gesturing to the two men on the ground, he said, "No wonder these two guys laughed when I asked if either of them were —"

"Keep still and your hands where I can see 'em!"

Indy lifted his hands high and said, "Easy, now. I was just looking for a pilot, not for trouble. *They* jumped *me*."

Bert glanced at the two men and then noticed the empty wine jugs that lay near them. "Dang," she said. "I only hired Tom and Jerry to watch the place while I was gone, not to get drunk and bust heads."

"Tom and Jerry?"

"That's right. The big one is Tomás, and the bigger one is Geraldo. They still breathing?"

"Yeah."

"Then I guess there's no harm done," Bert said as she holstered her gun and walked slowly toward Indy. A short tangle of brown hair stuck out from under her helmet, which framed her slightly sunburned features. She had hazel eyes and a thin but slightly crooked nose with a small bump across the bridge, evidence that it had once been broken. "You say you wanna go to Costa Rica? Whereabouts?"

Indy lowered his hands. "Palmar Sur, a river town in the

Osa region. I need to get to a banana plantation run by Amalgamated Fruit Industries."

"I know where the Osa is," Bert said. "But I never heard of Palmar Sur."

"I've got a map."

"Show me."

Indy took the map out of his bag and handed it to Bert. Bert gave a low whistle through her teeth and said, "Palmar Sur is a ways. About three hundred miles. And this map doesn't show me where exactly to land."

"I have American dollars."

"That's the only kind of money I know. But keep in mind I don't intend on staying in Costa Rica. You'll be paying for my flight back here, too."

"How much?"

Bert licked her upper lip, then said, "Three hundred dollars."

Indy lifted his eyebrows. "Three hundred? I don't want to *buy* the plane."

Bert smiled but her gaze went steely. "That insult won't cost you, mister," she said. "But if you even think of trying to haggle, my price jumps to four hundred."

Indy grimaced, then said, "Okay." He reached into his jacket's pocket slowly so Bert could see he wasn't removing a weapon, and took out the money-filled envelope he'd appropriated from Nichols. He dipped into the envelope and removed six fifty-dollar bills, then returned the envelope to his pocket. Handing her the money, he said, "How soon can we leave?"

After stuffing the bills into a pocket, Bert consulted her wristwatch and then glanced at the sky. "No point in leaving right now," she said. "It'll be dark in a few hours, and I don't like flying in the dark."

"It doesn't get dark *that* early," Indy muttered.

"Early enough for me."

"Would another fifty dollars change your mind?"

"No," Bert said. "But another hundred will."

"Done," Indy said bitterly. After he gave Bert the money, he picked up his whip and duffel bag. Tilting his head at the prone figures behind him, he said, "What about Tom and Jerry?"

"They can sleep all they want. They're fired." Bert turned and started walking toward the waiting plane, not even glancing at her clean shirts and trousers that dangled from the line as she brushed past them.

Indy followed Bert Brodowski to her plane. He liked the way she walked, but knew better than to say so.

Bert Brodowski's biplane was a 1930 Stearman C-3B with a refurbished 220 horsepower Wright Whirlwind J-5 engine. She had installed extra fuel tanks to give the plane a range of almost 550 miles and, because she had topped off her tanks about an hour before she'd met Indiana Jones, their flight from Panama to Costa Rica did not require any stops.

Indy did his best to enjoy the aerial views of rolling mountains and mist-shrouded forests while trying to ignore the stiffness in his legs that came with the long ride. As the biplane approached the outskirts of Palmar Sur, Indy had no difficulty sighting the banana plantations that had been carved out of the forests below. Countless trees had been cleared, dirt roads had been made, and various shacks dotted the land-scape. On the roof of one large building, someone had painted a circular symbol around three banana-yellow letters: *AFI*, the insignia of Amalgamated Fruit Industries. Even though it was late in the day, laborers were still visible, loading bananas onto waiting trucks. He also saw a wide, dirt field on which over a dozen trucks were parked, along with a wide-winged, unpainted metal biplane.

Bert saw the AFI insignia, too. "Looks like we found your destination!" she shouted from the cockpit behind Indy as she angled for the dirt field. "Hang on! It's gonna be bumpy!"

Indy clenched his teeth and braced his body as Bert brought the Stearman down on to the field, but was imme-diately relieved that the landing wasn't as jarring as he had expected. Bert guided her plane to a stop a short distance from the wide-winged plane that Indy had noticed from above. According to the plane's insignia, it was a mail carrier. The parked trucks bore the Amalgamated Fruit Industries insignia.

After Indy and Bert climbed out of the plane, Indy said, "Thanks for the lift."

Bert shrugged. "You paid for it."

Indy had transferred the box that contained the small stone sphere to his satchel, which also held the gold figurines as well as his few supplies. As he put on his gun belt and secured his whip so it was displayed openly, he noticed a cluster of small buildings beyond the parked trucks. He assumed the buildings were owned by Amalgamated Fruit Industries, and wondered whether Nichols had recently contacted anyone at the company. For all Indy knew, Nichols and Musgrove were already on their way to Palmar Sur.

A group of laborers beside a truck had noticed the arrival of Bert's plane, and Indy saw them looking in his direction. Indy returned his attention to Bert and said, "When will you be leaving?"

Glancing at the sky, Bert said, "It's already getting dark." She aimed a thumb at the other plane and said, "If I can find that mail crate's pilot and figure out how to refuel tonight, I'll leave in the morning. Why, are you looking for another ride?"

"I could be," Indy said.

"You're going back to Panama?"

"Beats me," Indy said. "I'm just letting destiny take its course."

Bert bit her upper lip, then said, "I'll wait for you, but I won't wait for free."

Indy gave Bert a ten-dollar bill and said, "I'm going to have a look around, but I should be back soon. Here, take this, too." He held out his empty duffel bag.

Taking the bag, Bert said, "What am I supposed to do with this?"

"I don't know. Fill it with bananas."

"I don't like bananas."

"Then use it for something else."

Leaving Bert, Indy walked over to the laborers and found a mustachioed Costa Rican who appeared to be in charge of the group. Because Indy didn't want to alert the local authorities to his presence, he introduced himself as a Canadian geologist, then asked if the stories he had heard about the discovery of strange stone spheres were true.

"*Sí*," said the man.

"*¿Qué distancia hay a las Tres Hermanas?*"

"*No está lejos.*"

Glad to learn that the stones known as the Three Sisters weren't far away, Indy asked if he could hire the man as a guide. The man eagerly accepted, and gestured for Indy to climb into the truck.

*   *   *

It had taken some time for Colonel Musgrove and Major Nichols to make their way back to the army air force base, where they immediately spearheaded a search for the elusive Dr. Jones. This had not gone over well with the base's commanding officer and everyone else who had been under the impression that Jones died earlier that day.

Suspecting that Jones might be headed for Panama City, Musgrove alerted the authorities there and ordered a series of roadblocks. As much as Musgrove and Nichols had been eager to move on to Costa Rica, they saw no point in doing that without the stone sphere "key," which Jones now possessed.

As darkness fell, Musgrove and Nichols sat in an office at the base, waiting impatiently for any report of Jones's whereabouts. Both of them looked up from their seats when Corporal McGuinness walked into the office, faced Musgrove, and said, "I think we might have something, sir."

"What is it?"

"At our roadblock at Santa Clara, we just picked up an old man in a pickup truck."

Nichols leaned forward in his chair. "Was Jones with him?"

"No, sir. But the old man was wearing a sergeant's shirt that's definitely too big for him. Would either of you know anything about that?"

Twenty minutes later, the man in question was delivered to the base. Corporal McGuinness and two military police officers escorted the man to the office where Musgrove and Nichols were waiting. Musgrove immediately identified the man as the same one whom Indy had referred to as "the Hammer." The confused man was frightened by the American soldiers, and did not hesitate to tell Musgrove and Nichols the location of the airfield where he had dropped off Indiana Jones.

"That's Bert's place," Corporal McGuinness said. "It's about a forty-minute drive from here. Bert's a lady pilot, flies her own biplane."

"You have a record of the model number?" Nichols asked.

"Yes, sir."

"Good," Musgrove said. "Get some men over to that airfield pronto and alert our contacts at Amalgamated Fruit Industries in Costa Rica. I want every airport within a thousand miles to know about that biplane. It's imperative that we find Dr. Jones, and tell everyone I want him alive and unharmed."

McGuinness and the MPs escorted the old man out of the office, leaving Musgrove and Nichols alone. Nichols said, "Jones may have run out on us, but I'm betting he hasn't abandoned the mission. Mark my words, sir, he's taking the stone to Costa Rica. We should leave immediately —

and we should bring troops with us, just in case we need them."

"Troops?" Musgrove said. "Hang on. What if Jones is misdirecting us again, like he did at the cantina? Maybe he's hiding somewhere in Panama, or traveling by car. I want to confirm that he's no longer at that airfield before we go flying off anywhere."

"I really don't think Jones would have stuck around," Nichols said. "It's not in his nature. I'm telling you, we're wasting time if we stay here."

Musgrove closed the office's door so he couldn't be overheard, then looked back to Nichols and said, "Have you forgotten the possibility of Nazi spies monitoring us? If the Nazis *did* send that assassin to stop Jones from finding the Hall of Records, maybe they're still keeping track of *us*. If we leave now, we might wind up leading them straight to Doctor Jones again."

Trying to remain composed, Nichols said impatiently, "Sir, if *we've* figured out that Jones was last sighted at a private airfield in Panama, it's possible that Nazi spies have learned the same thing. For all we know, they're already after him!"

Musgrove considered this, then said, "I'm willing to take that chance. Jones seems to work just fine on his own, and after all the trouble we've caused him, I can't blame him for wanting to steer clear of us." He walked over to a window and gazed out at the night sky. "We'll let him have his head start, and we'll fly to Costa Rica in the morning."

"That's not possible, sir," said Nichols from behind him.

Turning his gaze from the window, Musgrove said, "Why not?" As he turned, he suddenly noticed the small automatic that had appeared in Nichols's hand. In that same instant, Nichols pulled the trigger.

Musgrove felt the bullet slam into his chest and flung his hands up to clutch at the wound. He stood gaping at Nichols for a moment, but then his knees buckled and he collapsed to the office floor.

Nichols returned the automatic to his shoulder holster as he stepped over Musgrove's body, and then he opened the window that Musgrove had been gazing through less than fifteen seconds before. As approaching footsteps sounded from beyond the office's closed door, Nichols dropped to kneel beside Musgrove. A moment later, from outside the door, a voice shouted, "Colonel Musgrove?"

"He's been shot!" Nichols shouted back.

The door burst open and two MPs burst into the office with their guns drawn. Nichols gestured to the window that he had just opened and said, "Hurry! The shot came from outside!"

One MP ran to the window but the other crouched down beside Musgrove and felt for a pulse. "He's breathing," the MP said to Nichols. "I'll get him to the infirmary!"

Nichols reacted with a scowling expression. The MP saw this and assumed that Nichols was angry because someone had tried to kill Musgrove. The MP was wrong. Nichols was angry because his mission would have been easier if Musgrove were already dead.

CHAPTER EIGHT

*I*ndy's Costa Rican guide was called Enrique, and he turned out to be a most talkative fellow. He told Indy all that he had heard about the strange stone spheres. Apparently, no one knew the stones' age or origin. Some claimed the stones were made by ancient people, others said they were the result of volcanic phenomena. Then there were those who had believed that the stones contained pure gold or precious gems, and so they had drilled and dynamited a good number of stones to find out the truth. So far, none of the stones had yielded treasure.

As the truck's headlights illuminated the wide path that had been cut through the forest, Indy scowled with anger at the thought of any spheres being destroyed because of sheer greed. He didn't know how to use the "key" stone in his possession, and hoped it hadn't been engineered to work on one specific stone. If that stone had already been blasted to bits, he had traveled a long way for nothing.

Enrique steered the truck onto a field and came to a stop. In front of the truck, the twin beams of the headlights projected onto the surfaces of three immense stone spheres that rested on the ground. The Three Sisters were positioned just a few feet away from each other in a triangular arrangement. Indy thought they looked like a gathering of fallen moons.

Indy asked Enrique to wait for him, then he climbed out of the truck, taking his satchel with him. He had shoved his leather gloves into one jacket pocket, and he put the gloves on as he stepped over to the spheres. When he stood beside the largest sphere, he examined its surface up close. He had hoped to find a small hole that might accommodate the marble-sized "key" he had brought, but, except for a few weathered cracks here and there, the large sphere did not appear to have anything resembling such a keyhole. He moved around the other spheres, inspecting them as well, and found their surfaces to be similarly solid. For a moment, he found himself imagining the ancient artisans who had crafted the spheres. His best guess was that they were pre-Columbian.

Indy reached into his satchel and removed the metal box that contained the stone key, then opened the box carefully to reveal the small sphere within. He had not touched the stone since it had first been presented to him, and he didn't know whether his gloved hand would in any way inhibit the illusion of Atlantis that the stone projected. There was only one way to find out. He took a deep breath, then cautiously tapped the stone with his gloved fingertip.

Indy was relieved that his mind remained clear, without any invasive vision of Atlantis.

He exhaled, then glanced back over his shoulder to confirm that Enrique was still seated within the truck. Enrique wasn't even looking at him, but was casually staring out the window in a different direction. Still, Indy shifted his body so Enrique would not be able to see what he was about to do.

He removed the key stone and held it close to the largest sphere. And he waited.

Seconds passed. Nothing happened.

Feeling slightly foolish because he had no clue about what he was doing, Indy carried the small stone over to one of the other spheres. He waited there for a minute, and then pressed the key stone directly against the sphere. He thought, *This really isn't working.*

Not knowing what else to do, he turned to carry the key stone to the third sphere. But as he stepped into the central area between the Three Sisters, the key stone became suddenly warm in the palm of his left gloved hand. Indy looked down and saw that the marble-sized sphere was glowing brightly.

Indy watched the glowing sphere with wonder, but some strange instinct told him he would have to touch the small sphere with his bare hands. Holding the sphere steady in his left glove, he raised his right hand to his mouth and bit gently at that glove's fingertips so he could pull his hand free. As he extended his right index finger toward the glowing sphere, he thought, *How is this supposed to help me find the Hall of Records?*

The instant his fingertip came in contact with the glowing sphere, Indy's mind was flooded by fantastic images and sounds. A cascade of brilliant colors that crashed like ocean waves. Rippling explosions that sent blazing particles in all directions. Innumerable spheres hurtling through space. Columns of light that rose to infinity. He shuddered at the overwhelming visions and wondered how much more he could tolerate when a massive pyramid-shaped tower appeared before him, rising up from the jungle floor.

The tower was a Mayan step pyramid, a stonework ziggurat with a rectangular base, terraced stories, and two temples at the top. Unlike most pyramids, it had rounded sides and was set on a massive rectangular base. As the tower suddenly loomed above Indy, he was unaware of any glyphs within his visual range or the sound of an instructive voice, and yet the place's name and location somehow instantly instilled themselves within his mind.

Although Indy had never visited the site before, he realized he was familiar with it because he had read about the Danish archaeologist Franz Blom's excavations there just a few years earlier. But before he could contemplate that memory further, a doorway appeared at the lower side of the pyramid and began to glow.

And then he knew that the doorway was the entrance to the Hall of Records.

Indy pulled his fingertip away from the glowing sphere. He gasped as his vision of the pyramid vanished.

Wondering if Enrique had witnessed anything unusual, Indy quickly turned to look back at the truck. Enrique was still looking off in a different direction, but now rested his elbow on the edge of his door's open window, and had begun to drum his fingers on the window's edge.

He didn't see a thing. Indy carefully returned the key stone to its metal box and placed it in his satchel. As he surveyed the Three Sisters, he tried to comprehend the information that they had conveyed directly into his mind. He couldn't begin to imagine how the spheres functioned, but as he staggered back to the truck, he was not contemplating their ancient and possibly mystical technology. He was thinking about Brooksbank's warning about Nazi spies, and where he had to go next.

Indy couldn't explain it but thanks to the Three Sisters, he was certain of the current location of the Hall of Records. And it wasn't in Costa Rica.

"You want to go *where*?" Bert said.

"Uxmal," Indy said.

"Oosh-mahl?" Bert echoed.

"Yeah, Uxmal," Indy said. "It's in the Yucatán, about forty-five miles south of Mérida. There's a Mayan pyramid there. It's called the Pyramid of the Sorcerer. I read about an archaeologist excavating at Uxmal a few years back, and I'm just dying to see the place."

"Well, who wouldn't want to go to a place called Oosh-mahl?"

Indy wasn't sure if Bert's reply was sarcastic, so he decided to ignore it. He said, "Did you refuel while I was gone?"

"As a matter of fact, I did, thanks to the mail-carrier pilot who must have taken a liking to my smile, because the conceited jerk was compelled to tell me at least three times that he flies out of here in the morning. But just because my tanks are full doesn't mean I'm flying off to Mexico with you. I mean, shucks! The Yucatán Peninsula is a thousand miles away!"

"Not quite," Indy said. "It's just about nine hundred to Uxmal."

"Maybe as the crow flies," Bert said, "but I ain't a crow."

"Can you get me there?"

"Of course I *can*, but why *should* I?"

"I'll pay for your time, fuel, and your flight back to Panama."

"Well, doesn't that sound just easy as pie?" Bert said. "Tell me, are you *made* of money?"

"No," Indy said. "I just really need to get to the pyramid at Uxmal. It's important."

"How important?"

"Maybe fate-of-the-world important."

"Fate of the world?" Bert fixed Indy with a harsh stare, then said, "I've known all kinds, Jones, but I can't figure you out. So far, you've paid your bills on time, but a little voice inside my head tells me you're more than just a caution. You're a hazard waiting to happen. And I'm not flying you anywhere unless you tell me what you're up to."

"If I told you, you wouldn't believe me."

Bert put her hands on her hips. "Try me."

Indy considered his options, then said, "All right. I'll tell you, but not here." He glanced back at the truck that had carried him to and from the Three Sisters, and saw that Enrique was still behind the wheel. Returning his gaze to Bert, he said, "My new friend Enrique told me there's an inn nearby where we can get some food that won't make us sick."

Bert gave Indy a slightly puzzled look, then said, "Is that how you ask a lady out to dinner?"

"Yeah, Bert," Indy said. "That's how I ask."

*   *   *

The inn that Enrique recommended was little more than a series of attached shacks with a dining deck and some tables and benches, but food was indeed served, and Indy was able to reserve two rooms for the night. Lush foliage surrounded the deck, which overlooked a river. Indy and Bert found a table for themselves away from the other customers. As their late dinner was placed in front of them, Bert said, "What's the deal, Jones?"

"My friends call me Indy," Jones said as he cut into the poached fish on his plate.

Bert picked up a piece of meat and popped it into her mouth. "I'm still listening, *Jones*."

Indy chewed some food. "You want the long or short version?"

"*Reader's Digest* is fine by me, so long as the stories are true."

"Well, you asked for it," Indy said as he put his knife down beside his plate. "I'm a college professor and archaeologist, and I was on a dig in Peru when I was framed and then shanghaied by two guys from U.S. Army Intelligence. They wanted me to find something that they think is important, not just historically important but also scientifically. Unfortunately, the Nazis want this thing, too. Am I going too fast for you?"

"Not yet."

"Good. So, when my two army recruiters and I stopped to refuel in Panama —"

"You stopped at the base in Río Hato?" Bert interrupted.

"That's right. And I hadn't been there for more than twenty minutes when a total stranger with a German knife came out of nowhere and tried to kill me. Because I knew *I* hadn't told any assassins that I would be in Panama, I figured there was a leak of some kind. I also figured that the best way to avoid becoming a target was to part ways with Army Intelligence and proceed on my own."

"Wait," Bert said. "Back up there."

"Where exactly?"

"To the guy with the knife. He attacked you on the base?"

Indy nodded.

"How'd he get onto the base with so many guards all over it?"

Indy sighed, then said, "I know it sounds crazy, but I have a hunch he snuck in on the same plane I came in on."

"Really?"

"Yeah."

"What happened to him?"

"One of my recruiters shot and killed him before I had a chance to get any answers out of him."

"Huh," Bert said. "Now, back to the part about how you decided to proceed on your own."

"What about it?"

"By 'proceed,' you mean you're still on the mission that the Army wanted you to do? Chasing down this mysterious something you still haven't told me about, only you're doing it without the army?"

"That's right."

"Why?"

"I told you," Indy said grimly. "It's important."

Bert leaned back in her chair and eyed Indy levelly. "I'll give you this, Jones. I didn't read that one in *Reader's Digest*."

"I *told* you that you wouldn't believe me . . ."

"No, really, I am impressed," Bert continued. "I thought I'd heard them all."

"Everything I told you is true," Indy muttered.

"True, huh?" Bert put her elbows on the table and her hands under her chin, then leaned forward and said in a low voice, "I'll tell you something true, Jones. You're the first man I've met in a long time who didn't ask if 'Bert' was short for Roberta or Bertha, how my nose got broken, or how I wound up in Panama with my own biplane."

Indy shifted in his chair. "Is that good or bad?"

"Oh, that's good," Bert said with a gentle smile. "Usually, I get asked those questions within one minute of meeting anyone. But not by you. It made me think that you were different."

Indy shrugged, then leaned forward, too. "It's not that I didn't wonder," he said. "Maybe I just don't like asking obvious questions, at least not out loud."

Bert smiled more brightly. "What is it your friends call you again?"

Indy grinned sheepishly. "Indy," he said. "It's short for Indiana."

"That's cute," Bert said. "My name's short for You're-Full-of-Beans, Jones."

"Huh?"

Her smile was gone and Bert pushed her chair back from the table. "I said you're full of it. I don't care how much money you have. You're crazy and you can find yourself another way to Mexico."

Indy suspected that Musgrove and Nichols might already be on their way to Costa Rica, but he wasn't in any hurry to be back in their company. "Wait!" he said desperately, as Bert rose from the table. "Please, Bert. Just give me one more minute. I can prove it to you." He had brought his satchel with him to the inn, and Bert watched as he reached into the satchel, removed a small metal box, and placed it on the table.

Bert lowered herself back into her chair and eyed the box warily. She said, "If there's an engagement ring in there, I swear I'll knock you into next week."

"No ring," Indy said. He opened the box to reveal the small stone sphere within and gently pushed the box across the table.

Looking at the sphere, Bert said, "*This* little ball is the thing that the Nazis are after?"

"Not exactly," Indy said. "Actually, I forgot to mention this item. Just touch it."

Bert sighed, rolled her eyes, then extended a finger and touched the sphere.

Indy watched Bert's eyes go wide as her body went rigid. She appeared to be gazing at something behind him, but judging by her astonished expression, he knew she wasn't looking at the menu posted on the wall.

Bert yanked her finger away and nearly fell out of her chair. Righting herself, she looked at the sphere with amazement, and then lifted her gaze to Indy.

Indy kept his eyes on Bert's as he closed the box and returned it to his satchel. He said, "What do you think now?"

Blinking her eyes, Bert said, "I think you better start that story again. But this time, don't spare any details."

"It's late," Indy said with a yawn. "I'll tell you on the way to Uxmal."

Bert scowled and said, "No fair."

"I'm tired, Bert."

"So am I, Indy, but that's no excuse."

Indy cupped a hand beside his ear and said, "What's that? Did you just call me Indy?"

"Big deal," Bert said. "You'll probably have a new name for me when I tell you how much the flight to Mexico is going to cost you."

CHAPTER NINE

*I*ndy, wake up!" Bert shouted as she charged into his room at the Costa Rican inn.

"Wha —?!" Indy said as he sat up in bed and saw Bert. She was wearing her aviator helmet with her goggles pushed up across her forehead. Indy blinked his eyes and glanced at the window. "What time is it?"

"Almost dawn," Bert said. "An incoming plane woke me up, so I went out to check my Stearman. There are army soldiers all over!"

"Army?!" Indy muttered. "Whose army?"

"Would you believe the US of A?"

Indy got out of bed and began putting his clothes on. "Musgrove and Nichols must have tracked me here."

"Who're they?"

"The men from Army Intelligence I told you about," Indy said. "The recruiters I left behind."

"Well, they have soldiers guarding my plane, and I doubt very much they'll just let us leave the way we came." As Indy pulled on his boots, Bert added, "You really don't trust the Army Intelligence boys?"

"Neither of them has given me any reason to," Indy said as he rapidly laced his boots. "But I don't trust one in particular."

While Indy put on his hat and grabbed his gear, Bert said, "Where are you going?"

"I already told you," Indy said as he secured his gunbelt. "To the Yucatán."

"I want to help you, Indy, but I'm not leaving here without my plane."

"Fine," Indy said. "I'll figure out another way to get there."

Indy headed for the door. Bert followed him out of the room and onto a porch that wrapped around the back of the inn. A short flight of steps that was lined with potted plants led from the porch to the ground. Indy and Bert were halfway down the steps when a man's voice called out, "Dr. Jones!"

Indy stopped so suddenly on the steps that Bert bumped into him. He looked down to his right, through the leaves of a large potted plant, to see four American soldiers. Each soldier held his rifle so that the barrel was aimed high over Indy's head. Indy was wondering which soldier had called out to him when another man moved out from behind the soldiers to reveal his presence. Indy felt his anger rise at the sight of the man.

"A man named Enrique told us where we could find you," Nichols said. "I'm through playing cat and mouse with you, Jones. You're coming with us."

Indy didn't budge. "Where's Musgrove?"

"Lying unconscious in the infirmary at Río Hato," Nichols said evenly. "There was another assassination attempt at the airbase. I was with Musgrove when someone shot him through an open window."

"Is that a fact?" Indy said flatly, so it didn't sound like a question. "First Brooksbank, then me, and then Musgrove. I've got to hand it to you, Nichols,"

Behind Indy, Bert said, "Who's Brooksbank?"

"I'll tell you later," Indy muttered, keeping his eyes on Nichols.

Nichols held Indy's gaze as he said, "Don't make me order these men to take you in, Jones."

Indy nodded at the soldiers and said, "Do they know who gives you *your* orders?"

Nichols said, "I don't know what you're talking about."

"I figured it out back in Río Hato. The guy who tried to stab me, he didn't sneak past the guards at any gates. Someone smuggled him in on *our* plane, and then let him loose on me.

I wasn't sure if that someone was you or Musgrove, but now I know. You thought I was unnecessary to your mission, and you wanted me out of the way."

The four soldiers who stood beside Nichols held their ground, but one of them flicked his eyes at Nichols. Nichols said, "You have quite an imagination, Dr. Jones. Have you forgotten that I'm the one who stopped that man from stabbing you?"

Indy shook his head. "You only rescued your own hide," Indy said. "When you saw McGuinness was going to help me, you stepped in and shot the guy before he could talk. There wasn't *that* much steam in the shower."

Baffled, Bert said, "Shower?"

"Later on," Indy replied. Still facing Nichols, he continued, "I'm guessing the only reason you didn't kill me and McGuinness was because that would have left more of a mess than you could weasel your way out of."

Nichols glanced at the soldiers and said, "He's obviously insane."

"Am I?" Indy said. "Why don't you let these men look for a secret compartment in your DC-2 that's big enough to conceal a Nazi assassin? Or let them confirm if Musgrove was shot by your own automatic?"

Indy looked each soldier in the eye, hoping that at least one of them might consider the possibility that he was telling the truth. He had no intention of engaging the soldiers in a gunfight, but he wasn't about to surrender to Nichols either. All four soldiers shifted their gaze to Nichols.

Nichols kept his eyes on Indy as he said, "Arrest him."

Indy sensed the soldiers were hesitant, but then one of them decided to obey Nichols's order and advanced toward the steps. Indy responded by shoving his foot hard against the base of the large potted plant beside him. As the plant began to tumble down the steps, he grabbed Bert by the arm and yanked her up the steps, tugging her back onto the porch and into the inn. Bert shouted, "What do you think you're doing?!"

"Running!" Indy snapped back at her. "Come on!"

As Bert ran after Indy, heading for a door that led to the inn's kitchen, she said, "I don't think I like Nichols!"

"Join the club!"

They bolted through the kitchen, much to the consternation of the inn's cook and her two helpers, and then burst out the back door and raced for the nearest trees. They ignored the shouts from behind and kept their eyes forward as they plunged into the forest. Dodging trees and ducking low-hanging branches, they heard rifle fire from the inn. Bert responded to the noise with a frightened yelp and Indy grabbed her wrist, pulling her after him up a hill and through dense foliage — but he had no idea that the foliage concealed a sheer drop from a ledge that loomed above the river.

Indy fell, taking Bert with him. They plunged into the cold water, which wasn't so deep that Indy could stop from hitting the river's rocky bottom. A rush of bubbles escaped Indy's mouth as Bert landed on top of him, but he held tight to her as he kicked his feet against the rocks to launch them both to the surface.

Gasping for air, they kept their heads low as they pushed their way through the water to reach the tall grasses that grew at the river's edge. They glanced nervously back to the ledge to see if the soldiers had followed them, but saw no one. Staying in the water, they began moving cautiously through the high grass, making their way slowly up the river and against its current.

When they reached a bend in the river, they climbed out of the water and moved swiftly to a shadowy grove of trees. Soaking wet, Bert said, "What's your next move, cowboy?"

"If I could think of anyone I could trust in Washington, I'd try to send a warning about Nichols," Indy said as he checked his satchel to make sure he hadn't lost anything. "But it's just too risky. He may have allies, and I don't need them coming after me, too."

"You're certain Nichols is a Nazi?"

"All I know about him is that he's not the All-American freckle-faced boy he pretends to be, even if the freckles are real."

"So what *are* you going to do?"

"My plans haven't changed. One way or another, I'm still going to the Yucatán."

Bert stared hard at Indy, then said, "Tell me something. What happens if you *don't* go to that Mexican pyramid?"

"I have no clue," Indy said. "But if the Nazis are after the same thing I'm after, I can't let them get to it first."

Bert sighed. "This 'thing' you're after . . . it's really that important?"

"I'll put it this way," Indy said. "Remember the small stone sphere I showed you last night? Imagine there's more of them. Lots more. Enough for every person who ever lived and ever *will* live. They're all in a place called the Hall of Records. Now imagine that some of these spheres can predict the future just as clearly and vividly as they can illustrate the past, and that the Nazis might try using these spheres to control the future."

Bert stared at Indy blankly, then said, "You're serious? About this Hall of Records?"

Indy replied gravely, "You wouldn't want the Nazis to have that kind of control, would you?"

"Of course not!" Bert exclaimed. "But now that I think about it, I'm not sure I'd want *anyone* to have control like that."

"Will you help me, Bert?"

Bert licked her upper lip and said, "I'm guessing my plane's still being watched. How're we gonna get you to Mexico?"

Indy said, "I have an idea. But it kind of depends on how fast our clothes dry, and whether the mailman is still in town."

Their clothes dried fast in the oppressive heat, but it took almost an hour for Indy and Bert to sneak back through the forest and arrive at the edge of the field where Bert had left her biplane. They moved quietly, careful not to draw the attention of the soldiers who were stationed around Bert's plane. Indy was relieved to see that they weren't the same soldiers who had accompanied Nichols to the inn.

Indy whispered, "I wonder where Nichols's plane is."

Bert whispered back, "You said he has a DC-2?"

"That's right."

Bert gave Indy a reproachful look and said, "A plane that size can't land in an itty-bitty field like this."

"I *know* that," Indy said. "I just wonder where it is, and how far he is from it."

"In case he tries to come after us?"

"Yup." Edging past some trees, Indy sighted the other biplane that he'd noticed on the field the night before. "Look," Indy said. "The mail carrier's still there. You see the pilot anywhere?"

"No," Bert said. "And thank goodness for that." She removed the goggles from her aviator helmet and handed them to Indy.

Indy removed his hat and put the goggles on over his eyes. "How do I look?"

"Incredibly stupid," Bert said as she examined the goggles on Indy. "But from a distance, you almost look like an incredibly stupid pilot."

"Nice," Indy said.

Indy started to put his hat back on but Bert said, "Oh, no, you don't. Pilots don't wear fedoras. Give it to me. I'll tuck it inside my jacket."

"Well, all right," Indy said. "But be careful with it." He adjusted his satchel's strap over his shoulder and then said, "All set? Let's go."

Indy led Bert away from the protective cover of the trees and strode out onto the field wearing an angered expression as he headed toward the mail carrier. Without breaking his stride, he glanced back at Bert and bellowed, "I don't *care* what that Major Nichols said! He's just stickin' up for you! You, chasin' off all over the place with some outlaw college professor! Why I ever gave you a second chance is beyond me!"

"Stop, Hank!" Bert shouted at Indy, for that was what she had decided to call him, but he kept walking. "Please, it's true! I only gave that man Jones a lift here! You ain't got no reason to be jealous!"

Indy stopped and whirled on Bert. "No reason? No reason?!" He whacked his satchel with his hand and said, "For all I know, I've been carrying your love letters to another man for the past three years!" Then he lowered his voice so that only Bert could hear, and he said, "Did we get the soldiers' attention?"

Bert glanced at the men who stood around her plane, but who were now gaping in stunned silence in her direction. "We've got their attention, all right," she answered in a hushed tone.

"Good," Indy said. "Now go get your plane started."

Bert stepped back from Indy, gave him a wide-eyed look, and exclaimed, "Well! I never!" Then she turned and stormed off toward her own plane, leaving Indy standing beside the mail carrier. While Indy pretended to inspect the mail carrier's tires, Bert caught the eye of one soldier, a sergeant, and said to him, "Thanks a million for busting up my life."

The sergeant said, "Ma'am, I don't know what —"

"Oh, I'm sorry, I didn't mean to take it out on you," Bert interrupted. "Sorry, I'm Bert Brodowski, the owner of this plane."

"Yes, ma'am, and I have orders to —"

"Yes, I know all about the orders," Bert said as she moved to her propeller and gave it a slow turn to allow any pooled oil to drain through the valves in her engine's cylinders. "Your Major Nichols has already apologized to me, and told me I'm free to leave, for all the good that does. But I gotta warn you, my fiancé over there — or maybe I should say my *former* fiancé — isn't exactly the forgiving type." Tilting her head toward Indy, she raised her voice as she said to the sergeant, "You wanna try explaining to that big dope over there that even lady pilots have to earn a living? That before yesterday, I'd never even heard of Indianapolis Jones?!"

"Indiana!" Indy shouted back.

"Oh, he's just so jealous," Bert said, shaking her head. "Now if you'll excuse me, I have to fly on back to Panama and tell my mother that the wedding's off."

"I'm sorry, ma'am, but I should check with Major Nichols before you —"

"No, please don't bother," Bert interrupted. "You bring that nice major out here, Hank is just going to make another scene." Then she turned to the other soldiers, smiled prettily, and said, "Thanks for keeping an eye on my plane, boys."

The soldiers watched in stunned silence as Bert climbed up into her cockpit. Indy glanced away from the mail carrier's tires when he heard Bert's engine turn over. The engine coughed twice before it roared to life, and then the plane started moving forward.

The plan was for Bert to make a wide turn on the ground before taking off, and as she swung by the mail carrier, Indy would hop on her plane's lower left wing and scramble into the forward cockpit. If they played it right, they'd be airborne before the watching soldiers figured out who "Hank" was.

Bert's plane began to swing around toward Indy. He was about to get ready to make a run for her wing when a voice behind him said, "Just what in Sam Hill do you think you're doin'?"

Indy turned around and found himself facing a tall, lanky man. Indy gaped, then said, "I was, um . . . are you the pilot of this plane?"

"I sure am!"

Hearing Bert's plane draw closer, Indy sighed and said, "Well, I've got to go now —"

"You ain't goin' anywhere!" the pilot snarled as he grabbed Indy by the shoulder.

"Aw, heck," Indy said as he sent his fist flying at the pilot's head. But the pilot was fast and he ducked the jab. Still gripping Indy's shoulder, the pilot brought his other fist up into Indy's stomach.

Indy groaned as he saw Bert's plane taxi by. He threw his arms around the pilot and fell sideways, letting his weight carry them both to the ground. Past the roar of Bert's engine, Indy heard one of the soldier's yell, "Fight!"

Indy wriggled out of the pilot's grip and tried to roll away, but he caught Indy by the ankle and Indy stumbled. Indy kicked at the pilot and scrambled up from the ground, but then the pilot sprang up and threw another punch at Indy. The punch glanced off Indy's upper arm and Indy hit the pilot right on the nose.

As the pilot howled in rage and pain, Indy looked aside to see that Bert was circling back again, driving the plane around the soldiers who had become spectators to the fight. Indy was wondering how many seconds would pass before Bert got close enough for him to jump on the wing, when the pilot drove his fist into Indy's ribs.

Indy winced at the impact, but whipped his left arm out so that his knuckles swiped the pilot's nose again, then launched his right fist up against the base of the pilot's jaw. The pilot's head snapped back but he didn't fall, and merely lowered his chin to stare at Indy with a dazed expression.

Aware that the soldiers were watching, Indy aimed a reprimanding finger at the pilot and shouted, "That's what you get for making eyes at my girl!"

The pilot looked at Indy quizzically and gasped, "Your girl? What're you talking ab —?"

Indy hit him again. The pilot fell back but somehow managed to snag one hand at the strap of Indy's satchel. Hearing Bert's plane edge closer to his position, Indy tore his satchel free from the pilot's grip and then turned around and got ready to jump.

Indy practically fell atop Bert's wing, but he grabbed hold of a metal brace and held tight. His feet dragged behind him before he hauled himself up on to the wing. The nearby soldiers glanced back and forth from Indy on the moving plane to the pilot he'd left defeated by the mail carrier.

Indy grabbed another brace between the wings and then maneuvered his body up and into the forward cockpit as Bert straightened out her course and increased speed across the field. Then the biplane lifted up and away, into the sky.

Indy gazed back at the airfield and saw one soldier run to the fallen pilot while the others ran off the field. His heart was pounding in his chest. He hadn't much enjoyed tricking the soldiers, but he did feel some satisfaction that he and Bert had managed to escape Nichols.

Indy shifted his satchel on to his lap and noticed the satchel had a tear along its side. He realized it must have torn open during his fight with the pilot, and then he muttered, "Oh, no."

As the wind whipped at his head and Bert guided her plane to the northwest, Indy opened the satchel to see if he had lost anything, and immediately discovered that he had. It was just one item, but it was the one he shouldn't have left behind.

Twenty minutes after Bert Brodowski's biplane had ascended from the field outside of Palmar Sur, Major Nichols learned of her dramatic departure and was so enraged that he nearly shot the sergeant who had delivered the news. Nichols remained furious for nearly fifteen minutes more, until he arrived at the field and found a group of soldiers standing around a somewhat bruised and disheveled pilot, who had somehow come into possession of a small metal box that Nichols recognized at once. The pilot said he believed the box belonged to the man who'd knocked him out, but warned Nichols not to touch the ball inside the box because it was "spooky."

"Thanks," Nichols said, as he took the box from the pilot. "I'll remember that."

Then Nichols turned to the nervous sergeant who had unwittingly allowed Dr. Jones to escape from Costa Rica, and he said, "Somewhere in the area, there are three large stone spheres called the Three Sisters."

"Yes, sir?"

"Find them for me. Now."

CHAPTER TEN

*I*ndy was fortunate that Bert was no stranger to the skies of Central America, and that she had a collection of aeronautical charts stashed in her Stearman. She knew a discreet place to land and refuel in Honduras, and then another place in Belize, about 220 miles shy of their destination. As much as Indy wanted to continue on to Mexico, he didn't protest when Bert insisted they rest in Belize for the night, for it was getting dark and they were both too exhausted to fly on.

Still, Indy kept kicking himself for having lost the stone sphere back in Costa Rica, and he hoped he wouldn't live to regret the overnight stop in Belize. For all he knew, Nichols had already recovered the sphere, taken it to the Three Sisters, and learned that the Hall of Records had relocated to the Pyramid of the Sorcerer in Uxmal. If that happened, and Nichols somehow managed to reach Uxmal first . . . Indy didn't even want to think about it.

Early the next morning, Indy and Bert flew out of Belize,

heading north. Almost three hours later, Indy was anxiously consulting one of Bert's charts when he spotted a group of ancient structures below. Pointing to the tallest structure, he shouted, "There it is!"

Bert followed Indy's gaze to see the Pyramid of the Sorcerer, which rose over 100 feet from the ground. She said, "Since when do pyramids have curved sides?"

Indy ignored the question as he scanned the area surrounding the structures, searching for any sign of U.S. military aircraft, specifically Nichols's DC-2. Seeing nothing but treetops and a few dirt roads, he shouted back, "Can you set us down near the pyramid?"

"Can a pigeon land on a dime?" Bert answered loudly. She guided the Stearman into a wide circle as she studied the terrain, then came down fast and low over a stretch of relatively flat earth that extended past a quadrangular building to the pyramid. Even though Indy had already come to trust Bert's piloting skills, he still held his breath as the plane's tires met the ground.

Bert brought the plane to a stop just a short distance from the base of the pyramid. After the plane's engine went silent, they climbed out of their respective cockpits. As Indy rubbed his legs to get his circulation going, Bert said, "Looks like we have the place all to ourselves."

"Looks that way," Indy replied noncommittally as he

took in his surroundings. An unseen bird squawked from a nearby tree.

A stairway lined with at least a dozen stone mosaic masks ascended the pyramid. Bert gazed up to the temples at the pyramid's top and said, "So this is the Pyramid of the Sorcerer? Who was the sorcerer, anyway?"

"If I remember the legend right, he was a dwarf who built the place overnight."

"A dwarf sorcerer, huh?" Bert said as she eyed the mosaic masks. "I bet he didn't look anything like Mickey Mouse in *Fantasia*. Just how old is the pyramid?"

"No one knows for sure," Indy said. "But what we're looking at is probably over a thousand years old and, contrary to the legend, construction was somewhat ongoing. The Mayans built new structures over old ones."

"Well, they sure let the place go to H-E-double-toothpicks," Bert commented. "So, what now?"

Securing his satchel over his shoulder, Indy answered, "I'm going inside to have a look around."

"Just like that? You want me to tag along?"

"No, I don't," Indy said as he turned to face Bert. "If Nichols comes to Uxmal, I want you to be long gone by the time he gets here. In fact, right now, I want you to fly straight to Mérida."

Lifting her eyebrows, Bert said, "And leave you?"

Indy sighed. "Now's not the time to go sweet on me, Bert."

"Who's sweet?" Bert replied with a scowl. "I just want to know if you're gonna pay me what I'm owed before I take to the skies!"

Indy rolled his eyes, then took out the envelope that contained the money he'd taken from Nichols. "I'm just keeping some of this in case I need it later," he said as he removed a few bills. "Here, you take the rest. Now listen, this is important. When you get to Mérida —"

Bert was counting the money when she interrupted, "There's over a thousand bucks here. I *knew* I should have charged you more than four hundred dollars for the flight to Costa Rica!"

"Please listen, Bert. At Mérida, go to the U.S. Consulate; it's near the Parque del Centenario. Let the consulate know you last saw me here, and warn them about Nichols. Maybe they can get word to Panama and notify Musgrove, if he's still alive. Can you remember that?"

Tucking the money-filled envelope into her pocket, Bert said, "Considering Mérida's all of forty-five miles away, I think my memory can handle it. But this pilot's keister needs a break. I'm going to stretch my legs for a few more minutes before I take off."

"Fine," Indy said. "Just don't take more than a few minutes."

Indy was about to turn and walk away when Bert said, "Given that this might be our big good-bye, I want to ask you something, Jones."

Back to calling me Jones again, Indy thought. He said, "Then ask it."

Her hazel eyes coolly fixed on Indy's, Bert said, "Do you tell all the girls to get lost, or just the ones with broken noses?"

Indy was surprised by the question. He let out a quiet exhale, then said, "You'll be more help to me in Mérida than here, Bert. As for your nose, I think it looks fine as is, just like the rest of you. And I'd like you to stay fine, so get out of here."

Bert grinned, then said, "When I'm done stretching my legs. So long, Indy."

Indy smiled in return, then turned and approached the pyramid.

Barely four minutes after he'd parted ways with Bert, Indy rounded the Pyramid of the Sorcerer to find himself facing it from the exact position he recalled from his vision at the Three Sisters in Costa Rica. Remembering the doorway that he'd seen in that vision, he moved closer to the pyramid's base, which was partially covered by leafy vines.

Where's the entrance? He knew it was there, somewhere beneath the rampant foliage. He grabbed a length of vine and tugged at it, pulling it away from the base to expose the massive stones beneath, and then he tugged away at another vine. He was about to reach for one more vine when he saw the four small, shadowy recesses that had been carved into the side of one of the large stones.

The four recesses were arranged in a rectangular configuration. Indy leaned closer to the stone. The recesses were different in shape, and yet each was somehow familiar. He pushed his fingers inside one of them, feeling its contours, and then he saw the faded etching between the recesses. The etching represented a feathered serpent, the deity Kukulcan.

Indy thought immediately of the four gold figurines that were stowed in his satchel. Kneeling on the ground, he took the figurines out of the satchel and removed their cloth wrappings to examine them. Then he stood up, lifting the figurines so he could compare their shapes to the recesses in the wall. He gasped. Even before he inserted the gold vulture into the vulture-shaped recess, he knew it would be a perfect fit, as were the lizard, fish, and ear of corn.

But the gold figurines were not merely ancient puzzle pieces. Like the small stone sphere he had lost in Costa Rica, they were keys. To Indy's amazement, the stone with the four recesses slid slowly back within the pyramid, producing only the slightest clicking sound of some concealed, ancient mechanism. Then the stone pivoted to reveal a shadowy doorway.

Indy had been surprised when he had discovered the

Mayan figurines buried at the Incan shrine in Peru, but now he felt flabbergasted. He had never imagined that the figurines might serve such a specific purpose in what had become his search for the Hall of Records. It all seemed like such an impossible coincidence.

Maybe it is *destiny*, Indy thought.

Indy walked through the doorway, leaving the figurines in their respective recesses. A flight of stone steps descended to a dark chamber with a lofty, undecorated ceiling that appeared to be about twelve feet high. The chamber's only illumination came from the doorway behind him, but the light did not reach any of the chamber's walls. He tried to let his eyes adjust to the darkness, but when he was still unable to see beyond several feet, he knew he would need some kind of torch to proceed. He was about to turn for the steps and doorway to go looking for some dry wood when the air within the chamber began to hum.

Indy looked up to the ceiling and saw it appeared to be rapidly rising away from him. *Or is the floor descending?* He glanced back at the doorway, and saw that it was still there, the light pouring in from outside and down the steps.

Before Indy could comprehend what had happened, countless pinpoints of light appeared all around and above him. At first, they resembled distant stars against the darkness, but their fixed positions indicated an organized distribution, and when Indy shifted his body slightly, he realized some were within his reach. The closest ones looked like tiny orbs, illuminated from within.

He cautiously raised one hand and extended his index finger to an orb.

Inexplicably, Indy suddenly viewed a battlefield outside an English castle. Armored knights were fighting all over the place, and many lay dead or dying while a fire raged from the castle's highest windows. The smells of smoke and death were almost overwhelming. Indy heard a voice call out behind him, and his view swiveled to face a knight who was mounted on an armored horse and galloping straight for him. The oncoming knight raised a sword high over his head, and Indy felt an impending sense of dread when he saw sunlight glint off the sword's blade.

Indy gasped as he yanked his finger away from the orb, and saw that he was still standing amid the lights within the pyramid's cellar chamber. He thought, *The vision was so real, like going back in time and seeing it through someone else's eyes.* Although he couldn't comprehend the technology that enabled the orbs to store and convey such information, the experience had been painless. There was another remarkable aspect to the vision: The mounted knight's sword had looked strangely familiar.

Not at all certain of what might happen, he reached to another orb.

He saw a young boy, wading in a stream that snaked past the ruins of a castle. Indy realized it was the same English castle he'd seen in the previous vision. He didn't recognize the boy, but noted that the boy's shirt and rolled-up trousers were from a later period, possibly nineteenth century. The boy nearly stumbled in the stream, then he bent down to pick up something from underfoot. The boy had discovered a lost sword lying in the stream. It was the very sword that the mounted knight had wielded, only it was obviously older, the blade having lost its shine centuries earlier.

Indy removed his finger from the orb, then touched another.

"Junior! What do you think you're doing?"

Indy jumped at the sound of his father's voice, and then he was stunned to see Henry Jones, Sr., looming above him like a giant, a *young* giant with dark hair.

Indy held a large, heavy, tarnished sword in his hands, and he and his father were standing outside his father's study in their home in Princeton, New Jersey. Incredibly, Indy realized it was the same sword the boy had found in the stream. The scent of stew wafted in the air, and Indy heard something clatter from the kitchen. He wanted to run there, where he knew he would find his mother, but instead he tilted his head back to look up and meet his father's gaze as he replied in a high voice, "It fell off the wall and I caught it, sir."

Indy thought, *That's not my voice!* But then he realized it was, for he was just a child.

Indy's tall father scowled, then reached out for the sword, and said, "Hand it over."

Indy let out another gasp as he removed his finger from the second orb. He'd almost forgotten the incident with his father's sword, which he had deliberately removed from its anchors on the wall so he could play with it. *How old was I then? Six?* Old enough to know that it would be a lie to say that the sword had fallen from the wall, but he had lied anyway, and felt so guilty about it that he never touched that sword again.

Indy surveyed a cluster of orbs, wondering what visions or memories they contained. The desire to reach out to them was great, far greater than his childhood temptation to play with a real sword. He extended his hand to one more orb.

Indy had a vision of Bert standing outside the pyramid. She wasn't alone. Nichols was right behind her, his automatic leveled at her head.

Indy shuddered as he pulled away from the orb to end the vision. *Was that the present or the future?* He wanted to exit the pyramid immediately to check on Bert and help her if necessary. But before he could search for the way out, someone to his left said, "Saw something nasty, did you, Indy?"

Indy turned and was astonished to see a man standing amidst the glowing orbs. The man was well dressed, with wavy blond hair and a thin mustache.

Indy said, "Brooksbank?"

"Welcome to the Hall of Records," Sir Reginald Brooksbank said with a relaxed smile. "I'm glad you're here. Impressive, isn't it?" His eyes flicked to an orb that seemed to dangle to his left. "All the countless secrets this place holds. Just watch your step. Trust me, you don't want to touch too many of these spheres at once."

Indy's brow furrowed. "I don't get it. I . . . I thought the Nazis blew up your car."

"They blew it up, all right," Brooksbank said. "I just wasn't in the car when they did it."

"Huh," Indy said, still stunned to see his old friend alive. "You kind of forgot to mention that in the movie."

Brooksbank winked and said, "I was right about that scar on your chin, wasn't I? Oh, and you can bet the bank that the Yankees will win the next World Series!"

"Why'd you do it, Brookie? Why'd you pretend to be dead? And how did you wind up here?"

"Can we talk outside?" Brooksbank said, gesturing to the open doorway. "I came in here with provisions for a month, but I really do need a breath of fresh air."

"We can talk right here," Indy insisted. "You know as well as I do we're in the Yucatán."

"Yucatán? Really?" Brooksbank grinned. "I'm sorry, Indy, I really didn't know where we were. The Hall of Records is most mysterious."

"I'm listening."

"I've learned a great many things about it, but I still don't know exactly how it works." Looking at some nearby orbs, he continued. "It yields information, but finding answers to specific questions is quite difficult. For example, I managed to learn that the Hall could transport itself from Bimini to another location, but I didn't know where. And you shouldn't touch more than one orb at a time. Also, I learned that if I left you a stone sphere and directed you to the Three Sisters in Palmar Sur, you would open the Hall's door for me, because I'd be unable to open it on my own."

"Hang on," Indy said, feeling more than a little overwhelmed. "Let me get this straight. The Hall of Records *carried* you from Bimini to Yucatán, and you rode it even though you didn't know where you were going, or how you'd get out?"

Brooksbank nodded. "Yes, that's right. Fantastic, isn't it? As far as I can make out, it has something to do with multiple dimensionality . . ."

Dumbfounded, Indy said, "I still don't get it. Why'd you pretend to be killed?"

Brooksbank sighed. "As you must be aware, I notified U.S. Army Intelligence about my find. But not long after I met Colonel Musgrove and Major Nichols, I learned that Musgrove was a Nazi spy."

"Musgrove?!" Indy exclaimed. "You learned that from the Hall of Records?"

"No," Brooksbank said. "Nichols told me. He's been secretly manipulating Musgrove for months, having him send false information to his Nazi leaders. Nichols was waiting for the right moment to arrest Musgrove, but after I learned that the Hall could be relocated, Nichols decided it was best — for security reasons — if the Hall left Bimini."

"Oh, no," Indy shook his head. "Oh, no, Brookie. You made a big mistake."

"How?"

"Musgrove isn't a Nazi. Nichols is."

Before the astonished Brooksbank could answer, two figures appeared in the doorway at the top of the steps. They were Bert and Nichols. Nichols had Bert's wrists pinned behind her back and his automatic braced against the side of her head.

CHAPTER ELEVEN

*H*ands up!" Nichols shouted as he steered Bert down the steps and toward Indy and Brooksbank.

Mouth agape, Brooksbank raised his hands. Indy could see the fear and anger in Bert's eyes, but despite his concern for her, he also knew there was little point in surrendering to Nichols. *He'll pull that trigger if I give him any chance.* Keeping his hands at his sides, Indy said, "I guess you caught an early flight, Nichols."

"Arrived over five hours ago," Nichols said as he continued to push Bert along in front of him. "Plenty of time to conceal the plane. Now raise your hands!"

"You're wasting your time," Indy said calmly, playing his bluff. "You should let the woman go and put that bullet in your own head right now." Tilting his chin slightly toward a nearby cluster of hovering orbs, he continued, "Thanks to the Hall of Records, I know who survives the day, and I know it isn't you."

Nichols tightened his grip on Bert as he stopped, just ten feet shy of Indy and Brooksbank. Nichols snarled, "Hands up or I'll kill her!"

Indy grinned and shook his head. "You won't kill her, Nichols. You'll skin her forehead, but you won't kill her. She'll live, you'll run up those steps and out of here, and you'll find yourself lost in the jungle in no time. A vulture will be picking your bones before sundown. Isn't that right, Brookie?"

Hands still raised, Brooksbank said, "*That* was the nasty vision you saw?"

"Yeah," Indy lied. "It was *very* nasty."

"Quiet!" Nichols shouted. "I'm claiming the Hall of Records for the Fatherland, and *you* will die!"

Indy said, "Is it all right if I close my eyes? Even though I know what happens to you, Nichols, I really don't want to see it again."

"Liar!" Nichols yelled as he rapidly shifted his hand to aim his automatic at Indy and fired.

But Indy had made his move, too, sending his body sideways as he seized his whip and launched its tip at Nichols. The gunshot and whip's crack sounded simultaneously. The whip struck Nichols's hand, causing him to drop the automatic and howl in pain as he reflexively eased his grip on Bert's wrists. Bert responded by leaning forward and kicking back with one foot, driving it sharply into Nichols's shin.

Indy heard a groan beside him, and turned fast to see

Brooksbank clutching at his chest where the fired bullet had struck him. Brooksbank collapsed to his knees.

Indy looked fast to Bert. Her hands free, Bert spun and drove one fist into Nichols's stomach, then the other into his face. Indy returned his attention to Brooksbank, dropping to his old friend's side and said,

"Brookie!" Indy said. "Talk to me!"

Brooksbank forced a smile, then gasped, "Sorry, Indy. The Hall of Records . . . never told me *this* would happen."

Indy glanced at Bert to see her knock Nichols to the floor. To Brooksbank, Indy said, "I'll get you out of here!"

"No," Brooksbank said. "Leave me. I'm . . . done for. Just don't let the Nazis . . ." Brooksbank's eyes closed and his head fell back. He was dead.

Indy looked away from Brooksbank to see Nichols push himself up from the floor. Nichols glared at Indy and said, "I will not die here! I won't!" To avoid the alleged fate that waited for him outside, he turned to run deeper into the chamber, and went straight into a tight cluster of glowing orbs.

The orbs began bursting as Nichols's body struck them, and as Nichols screamed, Indy suddenly remembered Brooksbank's warning about touching more than one sphere at a time. Although Indy had never really foreseen Nichols's death, he now saw the man's body being shredded by brilliant lights. Nichols shrieked, and then, in a flash, he was gone.

There was a rumbling sound within the chamber, and the ground began to shake as more orbs began to burst around the area where Nichols had been consumed. Indy saw the stone door begin to close. He looked to Bert and shouted, "Run for the stairs!"

Leaving Brooksbank's corpse, they bolted up the steps. As they ran, Indy saw the four gold figurines jouncing in the door's recesses, about to fall out. Thinking fast, he removed and inverted his hat, then shoved it under the figurines so that they fell into the hat. A moment later, he and Bert stumbled outside and the door swung shut behind them.

Breathless, Indy and Bert looked back to the pyramid. The entrance had been completely sealed. Bert gasped, still catching her breath, "You bluffed Nichols?!"

"Yeah," Indy said. Looking into his hat, he saw that he had only managed to catch three figurines: the lizard, fish, and ear of corn. He considered the lost gold figurine, then added, "But a vulture went after him anyway."

EPILOGUE

"I'm sorry about Brooksbank, and about the mess I dragged you into, Jones," Musgrove said.

"And I'm sorry you were shot," Indy replied. "You sure you're okay?"

"Well, I feel plenty foolish," Musgrove admitted. "If Nichols hadn't tried to kill me, I don't know that I ever would have believed he was a Nazi spy. I was lucky, all things considered," Musgrove said. "The bullet went right through me without hitting anything vital."

Indy lifted his drink and said, "Here's to luck."

They were sitting in the bar at a hotel near the U.S. Consulate in Mérida. It was two days after Indy and Bert had left the Pyramid of the Sorcerer, and Musgrove, still wearing bandages under his shirt, had arrived that morning. Musgrove said, "I feel like a blamed fool about Nichols. Just so you know, you were right about the DC-2 — Nichols did have a secret compartment for the man who tried to kill you in Panama."

Indy shrugged.

Musgrove stared for a moment at his glass of water on the table, then said, "Do you really think the Hall of Records is lost forever?"

"I don't know," Indy said. "The older I get, the less sure I am of anything."

"I guess I don't have to tell you these are rough times, Jones," Musgrove said. "The way things are going, I don't believe it's a matter of *if* the war overseas reaches America, but a matter of *when*. Army Intelligence could use a man with your skills. Our sources in Berlin tell us that the Nazi party's interest in the Hall of Records was never about reading the future — they're certain they will be victorious. They want weapons technology. They have come to believe that the Hall held ancient knowledge concerning incredible weapons. Will you help us?"

"I'm a teacher, not a soldier," Indy said. "But I'll think about it."

After his meeting with Musgrove, Indy went up to the hotel suite that Bert had taken for the week. Bert had washed her hair and gone shopping for new clothes, and was wearing a crisp white linen shirt with a pale green skirt when she greeted Indy at the door. "C'mon in," she said.

Walking over the threshold, Indy said, "This sure is different from your place in Panama."

"I'm different when I have money."

"Maybe that explains why you look like a different woman."

Bert grinned. "Is that good or bad of me?"

"Depends on your motives," Indy said as he took his hat off. "I told you I liked you as is, before you went and got all dolled up for me."

"Who said I got dolled up for *you*?"

Indy shrugged.

Bert smiled and said, "Well, enjoy the view while it lasts. Because when the money's gone, I don't know where I'll be next."

"Ah, money," Indy said. "That reminds me, you'll want to save some for this." He reached into a pocket, removed a slip of paper, and handed it to Bert.

Bert looked at the slip of paper and said, "What's this?"

"The 1941 World Series, straight from the Hall of Records," Indy said. "Keep it under your hat until just before the first game, and then place your bets. If my old friend Brooksbank was right, you'll be set for life."

"Honest?" Bert said as she studied the numbers on the slip. "How much are you gonna bet?"

"Nothing," Indy said. "I like the Dodgers too much."